Deanne Anders was reading romance while her friends were still reading Nancy Drew, and she knew she'd hit the jackpot when she found a shelf of Harlequin Presents in her local library. Years later she discovered the fun of writing her own. Deanne lives in Florida, with her husband and their spoiled Pomeranian. During the day she works as a nursing supervisor. With her love of everything medical and romance, writing for Mills & Boon Medical Romance is a dream come true.

From Midwife to Mummy

is **Deanne Anders**'s debut title

Look out for more books
from Deanne Anders
Coming soon

FROM MIDWIFE TO MUMMY

DEANNE ANDERS

MILLS & BOON

First published in Great Britain 2019
by Mills & Boon, an imprint of HarperCollins*Publishers*
1 London Bridge Street, London, SE1 9GF

Large Print edition 2019

ISBN: 978-0-263-07865-7

This book is produced from independently certified FSC™ paper to ensure responsible forest management. For more information visit www.harpercollins.co.uk/green.

Printed and bound in Great Britain
by CPI Group (UK) Ltd, Croydon, CR0 4YY

This book is dedicated to my parents,
Rev. and Mrs. J. A. Atkison, who
loved and supported me and made
sure I always knew I belonged.

And to Lucretia Lee, R.N.
The best Labor and Delivery nurse
I ever had the privilege to work with.
I can never thank you enough
for the gift of your mentorship.

And to Theresa Lee.
While you might not be my sister
by blood or adoption, you will always
be my sister of my heart.

CHAPTER ONE

DIM LIGHTS AND the sound of soft waves crashing against the shore had created an atmosphere of a calm retreat, but midwife Lana Sanders knew that her patient had long passed the point of caring.

"You're doing great," Lana said as she coached Kim through another contraction and watched the fetal monitor. She watched the fetal heartrate accelerate, then come down to its baseline. So far this had been a perfect labor.

"You're going to be late," Jeannie whispered to Lana as she arranged the delivery table.

"It won't be long now," Lana said, as much to reassure the labor and delivery nurse as well as her patient.

"Push. *Now.*" Kim ground out.

"Wait, I've got to get the camera!" Kim's husband Tom called out as he turned his back and started going through a duffle bag laid upon the bedside table.

"Wait?" said Kim. Her voice rose an octave and took on that gravelly sound that only a woman in transition, or one possessed, could reach. "What have you been doing all this time?"

"It's okay, Tom, we have a couple minutes," Lana said.

A deep growl escaped from Kim.

"Okay, maybe we don't," Lana said as she watched a circle of dark wet curls crown.

She positioned the delivery table so that it would be within easy reach, then undraped it, letting the protective covering fall to the floor.

"Kim, we've done this before, right?" Lana waited till she had Kim's attention. "The baby's starting to crown so whenever you're ready go ahead and push."

"Now!" said Kim, then took a fast breath.

Tom rushed to his wife's side and helped her get into position as she curled her body and pushed down. Lana watched as the couple worked together for their child. Kim's face was flushed and glowing with color as she concentrated on nothing but this moment—the moment she would bring a new life into the world.

It was both beautiful and heart-wrenching for Lana to watch this miracle.

"Take another breath," Lana said. "Is the contraction gone?"

"No," Kim said, before she took a deep breath then returned to pushing.

"Okay, Kim, I need you to listen to me," Lana said.

She waited as Kim looked up at her.

"Next push we're going to have a baby, okay?" Lana watched as both excitement and fear filled her patient's tired eyes. "You can do this. I promise."

Kim nodded her head and grabbed Tom's hand as she positioned herself again, then pushed.

Seconds later a screaming, squirming baby boy was delivered. Lana carefully suctioned the baby's mouth, then handed Kim her new baby and watched as the experienced mom caught him close against her body, putting him skin to skin to keep him warm while Jeannie dried him off with some fluffy towels. She clamped then cut the umbilical cord that had been the baby's lifeline. Seeing both mom and baby meeting for the first time, she was amazed, as always, by the miracle of life that she was blessed to witness.

"You did wonderfully," Lana told Kim.

Lana delivered the placenta, then made sure her patient's bleeding was controlled. A quick glance at the clock above the bed had her suddenly feeling a sense of panic. She had to get out of the hospital in the next twenty minutes or she was never going to make it to court on time.

She gave the new mom a hug, then posed for a picture with the rest of the Callahan family once they were allowed in the room. She headed to the nurses' lounge for a quick change of clothes, then headed out of the hospital. This was going to be one of the most important days of her life. Today she would officially become a new mom herself—something that until a year and a half ago she had thought would never happen.

There was no way she was going to be late.

Lana white-knuckled her way through the nightmare of Miami traffic. The multiple lanes all seemed to be going nowhere, and Lana was short on both time and patience. For the first time she was scared she really was going to miss her appointment with the judge who would be finalizing Maggie's adoption.

The thought of her sweet, adorable little toddler had her taking a deep breath and relaxing. It would be okay. She was cutting it close, but she would make it. After over twelve months of social workers' visits and court appearances, there was no way fate would fail her now.

It had been fate that had brought the little girl into her life, after Lana had just happened to take on her young mother as a patient. When Chloe had later decided she couldn't handle the responsibility of a new baby and showed up on her doorstep, handing Lana the child along with a notarized letter saying she wanted Lana to adopt her, it had been nothing short of a miracle.

A lane opened up to her right and she swung into it and followed it to the next exit. Fifteen minutes later she made it to the judge's chamber where her appearance was scheduled to be. She was surprised to see that neither her lawyer nor her babysitter and Maggie were outside the room, waiting for her. She had texted both of them to let them know she was going to cut it close.

A note on the door explained that there had been a change in where the session would be held. Lana rushed down the hall to the courtroom. As she reached for the handle of the door a large hand reached around her.

“Let me,” said a male voice in a slow drawl that almost curled her toes.

Lana turned and followed the outstretched arm up to the man behind it. The sight of coal-black hair curling around an angular face with a pair of deep blue eyes was startling. Forgetting that she was blocking the door, she let her gaze continue down the tailored black suit to the pointed toes of black leather cowboy boots peeking from beneath his pants leg.

A cowboy in Miami?

The thought had Lana smiling as she looked up at the handsome man and with a quick “Thank you” continued into the courtroom.

A frantic Amanda waved at her from the front of the courtroom, where she and Lana’s lawyer Nathan had taken their seats. As soon as Maggie got a look at Lana the toddler started protesting. She wanted to get down and see her "mama" right then.

Amanda had dressed her in the new pink sundress Lana had recently bought, and with her dark curls and big deep blue eyes she looked like a china doll come to life. Lana reached over and took her little girl. She gave her a big tight hug that had Maggie giggling and squirming in her lap.

"Why the change to the courtroom?" she asked Nathan as she scooted into the seat next to him.

"Shh…" Nathan whispered back as he studied some of the papers in his hand.

Amanda looked at the two of them, then shrugged her shoulders, letting Lana know that she didn't have a clue about what was going on.

Nathan was always a little uptight-looking, which Lana put down to his job in family law. She knew that sometimes his cases were very stressful, with emotions riding high, but there was something about the way he was studying the papers in his hands that told her something was wrong.

Suddenly her heart kicked into panic mode. It was the same feeling she had when she woke up in the middle of her repeated nightmare about Chloe showing up at her door and telling her that she had changed her mind. That she didn't think Lana would be a good enough mother for Maggie and she was taking her away. Taking the little girl Lana had fostered since she was six weeks old. Taking her far away to somewhere Lana would never see her again.

It was the same nightmare she'd had for months now, but after today it would surely go away. Once the adoption was final Lana would be Maggie's mother, just as if she had given birth to her. There would be no way anyone would be able to take her away then.

As Judge Hamilton entered the courtroom everyone rose, then sat when the bailiff indicated. Taking a second to look around the courtroom, Lana noted that the social worker, Ms. Nelson from the Florida Department of Children and Families, who had been handling her case, was seated on the right at the front of the courtroom. She watched as the older woman handed the bailiff some papers that were then given to the judge.

Apprehension sent a shiver down her back. Lana looked at her lawyer again, to see his attention glued to the judge, who was now reading over the documents the social worker had presented to him.

"This is the hearing for the final placement of the child known here as Maggie. I know that Maggie has been fostered with Ms. Sanders since..." Judge Hamilton paused as he read the documents in front of him "...since she was six weeks old, and that the child's biological mother personally requested that Ms. Sanders be allowed to adopt her daughter."

The judge looked up and gave Lana a smile. Lana felt the tension ease and relaxed back into her seat. Judge Hamilton had always been encouraging in her quest to adopt Maggie. She knew her case was in good hands as long as he was on the bench.

"Ms. Sanders has been forthcoming in all the demands the court has placed on her, and she has met every requirement that the Department of Children and Families demands."

Judge Hamilton once more picked up the documents. This was it—finally he would say the words she had been waiting for and Maggie would be all hers.

"To be clear, this was to have been the last

hearing and the adoption was to have become final today."

Was to have become final? Were they going to make her jump through another hoop today?

"Ms. Nelson, you have indicated in your request to postpone the adoption that you have some new information that needs to be considered. Is that correct?"

Lana watched the social worker as she rose and walked to the front of the court room. Glancing at her lawyer for some sign as to what was happening, she noted that there was no look of surprise in his eyes as he watched the judge and the social worker quietly discussing the new documents she had handed him. When Nathan turned and took Lana's hands his look of concern pierced her heart.

Only something truly wrong would cause that kind of reaction in Nathan.

Amanda reached for her other hand and, looking at her, Lana saw the fear that she knew mirrored her own. Maggie, thinking this was a game in which she was not included, pulled at the adults' hands and started babbling in her sweet baby voice.

Lana released her hold on the others and wrapped her arms around her little girl. Okay, so there was another delay. There had been several over the last year. They had managed to clear each hurdle to get to this point, and if there was something else the court wanted from her she could handle it.

"It has come to the court's attention that there is a new petition to stop this adoption by someone who claims to be a family member—a brother of the biological father," Judge Hamilton stated.

Lana's heart stuttered for a moment, then raced forward at a speed that had a gasp escaping into the quiet court room. She pressed Maggie closer to her chest as she felt the adrenaline rush hit her, telling her either to run or prepare to fight. She clasped Maggie tightly, needing to feel the reassurance that only physically holding her child in her arms could give her.

"Is the person petitioning the court present?" the judge asked.

Lana watched her nightmare play out in front of her as the cowboy she'd seen earlier rose to his feet.

"I'm Trent Montgomery, Judge Hamilton, and I have reason to believe that I'm Maggie's uncle."

Trent walked into the small room at the side of the courtroom and took a seat at the small rickety table. Across the table sat the young woman he had met going into the courtroom—the woman he now knew as Lana Sanders.

He was surprised he hadn't recognized her from the picture he had found among the items his brother had had when he was taken to the hospital. Of course the young woman pictured smiling at the toddler whose hand she held looked young and carefree, with her hair flying all around her face as a breeze blew through the blond strands, while the woman he had opened the door for was all business, in her tailored skirt and blouse and her hair pulled back in some sort of clip.

Now the woman had let her hair down in more than one way, and her bright green eyes shot daggers at him as she talked with an older woman with steel-gray hair and eyes to match. He had no doubt that at that moment she wanted nothing more than to come over to the table where he sat.

Not that he didn't understand the kind of anger she was feeling. When his brother's lawyer had contacted him about the child he had wanted to hit something—anything—just to be able to take out the anger he'd felt at his brother. How could his brother have kept it from him that he had a little girl?

The lawyer had stated that Michael hadn't believed the contents of the letter he had received from his ex-girlfriend. But when the private detective he had hired had brought back pictures of a smiling toddler with coal-black ringlets and bright blue eyes, he'd known that the child was his.

After the lawyer had read Michael's will, and left some pictures of the child, Trent had come to the same conclusion as his brother. The child could only be a Montgomery. Another Montgomery child that had been abandoned.

He'd looked at those pictures a lot during the last two weeks, as he had tried to decide what to do about the child. She looked happy, smiling at the pretty blond woman, who smiled back with a love that seemed to pour out of the picture.

Why would he want to take this child away from this woman who appeared to love her? And what did he know about raising a little girl? Sitting there across from a woman who plainly wished a hole would open up and swallow him, he wondered for the hundredth time why he'd uprooted his life to come somewhere he didn't want to be and where he certainly didn't have a clue about what he was doing.

But he would go through with it. Because his brother had asked him to take care of this child if something happened to him. And because the little girl was a Montgomery, and that made her his responsibility.

He had failed to keep his brother safe from his father's destructive influence, but he wouldn't fail this child. On paper, Lana Sanders looked like the perfect mom, but Trent knew better than to believe everything he read. He would protect Michael's child as he should have protected Michael.

Once the court awarded him custody of his niece he would pack up and head back to Houston, where he belonged. Somehow he would have to find a way to make things work till then.

"Lana, I want to tell you first that I know this isn't going to be easy for you. You've been taking care of Maggie for months now, and I know you love her very much. Second, you need to know that the court has to consider any interest the biological family has in Maggie." Ms. Nelson the social worker stated. "I've seen the letter they have from Chloe, telling Mr. Montgomery's brother about her pregnancy. And then, of course, there's the resemblance that none of us can deny."

"And where was this biological family when she was six weeks old with no one to take care of her?" Lana spat out.

She looked across the table at the man who had been sitting quietly as she had questioned the social worker. Those blue eyes that she had found so appealing earlier now seemed ice-cold as they followed her every movement. He might as well just be an onlooker into this catastrophe he had orchestrated. Her life had suddenly been turned upside down, and he acted as if this was just another meeting for him to attend. As if he had no interest at all in the outcome.

But then he shouldn't have any interest in her and Maggie's life. He shouldn't even be here.

The pain of her nails biting into her hands had her uncurling her fingers. So far she had managed to rein in her temper. Now, running her hands through her hair, she pushed it back from her face and wished she had left it up in the clip. She could feel the heat of anger in her face and she knew the sight of her reddened face and scattered hair couldn't be a pretty picture.

She would have to get herself under control before she reached panic mode. That was not something she wanted either of these two people in the room to see. Taking a deep, steady breath, she willed her body to relax. Turning back toward the social worker, she pleaded her case once more.

"What about when she was just born and she was going through withdrawal? Was there anybody from this so-called family interested in Maggie then?" Lana said, glad that she no longer heard a tremor in her voice.

"I'm sorry," Trent said. "I wasn't aware of

the child until a couple of weeks ago. If I had known I would have seen to it that my brother was here when she was born."

"And where is this brother of yours, huh? Why is it that you're here without him?" Lana asked. "If he's Maggie's father why isn't he here?"

Lana watched the man she had earlier thought of as cold turn glacial.

"My brother passed away three weeks ago."

The shock of the statement stunned her into silence. The man who was supposed to be Maggie's biological father was *dead*? She stared at the man sitting across from her, who had shown no emotion while discussing his brother's death. He was just full of bombshells, wasn't he?

"So why are you here? Why are you so interested in Maggie's life when apparently your brother had no interest at all?" Lana asked.

Turning toward the social worker, she noticed that the older woman had shown no reaction to this new information. Realizing that Ms. Nelson must already know about the death of the supposed biological father, she felt the relief of earlier fade.

"There is no way you can expect me to give

Maggie up to a man who isn't even her father. It's one thing to consider the father's rights, but this man is a stranger to Maggie. You have to see that Maggie is better off in a home where she feels safe and loved. That's why Chloe didn't take her. Why she left her with me. She wanted to make sure Maggie would always be in a stable home. She didn't want to ever have to worry that her baby was not being properly taken care of," she said as tears spilled from her eyes.

No way. No way would she let them take Maggie.

"We're not making any changes as far as Maggie is concerned until we investigate the situation, Lana," the social worker said as she took Lana's hand and squeezed. "The first thing we'll do is have a DNA test done on both Maggie and Mr. Montgomery."

"I'll give you the information you need to contact me," Trent volunteered.

"Thank you," the social worker responded. "And your lawyer has given us the information you have in relation to your brother's alleged paternity."

"And, having given you that information, I

would like you to consider allowing me some visitation with the child," Trent said.

"'The child' has a name. It's Maggie. And why should I let you anywhere near her?" Lana asked.

"It's your decision at this time, Lana, but we do have good reason to think that Mr. Montgomery's brother was Maggie's father," said Ms. Nelson. "And if the DNA tests come back to show Mr. Montgomery as being her uncle, he will be able to ask for visitation while the court decides on custody."

Lana looked at the man across from her. Cool blue eyes watched her from beneath thick dark lashes. She'd seen that calculating look before, only then it had been on the face of a toddler trying to figure out how to get another cookie after she had eaten her limit.

There was no denying the similarities this man shared with Maggie. And she feared that the DNA test would only confirm what her eyes were telling her now. Chloe had never said much about Maggie's father, but she had said she'd written him a letter telling him she was pregnant when she hadn't been able to get him to answer her calls. She had listed Maggie's father as "unknown" on the birth certificate when she hadn't heard anything from him, and she had refused to discuss him any further with Lana.

Lana rubbed at the tight knot she felt forming at the back of her neck. How could this day have gone so wrong? She was suddenly bone-tired. She knew she had to accept the fact that this fight wouldn't be won here today.

"I'll consider it," Lana said. "But if I agree, I will be present at all times."

"Thank you," Trent said.

"About the DNA, Mr. Montgomery… I'm sure your lawyer has made you aware that the results when testing for an aunt or uncle of a child will not be definitive. It will give us more of a likely match than proof of a biological relationship."

"Actually, it's *Dr.* Montgomery, Ms. Nelson. But please call me Trent."

For a moment Lana thought her brain would explode at this new piece of information. While she knew the court wouldn't show any prejudice as far as financial circumstances were concerned, it would surely still consider if a child's needs could be met. What if they felt that this Dr. Montgomery could provide better for Maggie?

"I'll contact you both after we receive the DNA results and set up another appointment," Ms. Nelson continued as she stood, letting Lana know that there wasn't anything else to be said today.

Lana stepped out of the room and drew her keys out of her purse with trembling hands. She was glad she had sent Maggie home with Amanda instead of having them wait for her. She would have to use the time it would take her to get home to get herself together.

Thank goodness she had found Amanda, a medical student, while she had been looking for a roommate. With Amanda able to fill in as babysitter in exchange for rent, she had the extra help that a single parent needed.

She'd go home and get Maggie into bed, call Nathan to see what her options were, and then she would come up with a plan. Dr. Trent Montgomery might think that he had everything going his way, but they said possession was nine-tenths of the law and right now Maggie was hers.

Lana had only been fifteen when she had

beaten the cancer that had been growing in her body. She'd lived through chemo and radiation treatment. She'd stumbled a bit when she had learned that the treatments that had saved her life had destroyed her dreams of having children, but she had managed to keep going even though she'd been hurting.

She was a fighter and she didn't give up. And she was about to make a certain cowboy wish he had never left Texas.

CHAPTER TWO

LANA WALKED OUT of LDR Four and headed for the OB nurses' lounge. The delivery had been complicated, due to the size of the baby boy, and the new mom had needed extra reassurance that everything was fine with both her and her baby. Now she would have to hurry back to the office as soon as she'd finished signing off on her orders.

She could hear the whispers and laughter of the nurses as she turned the corner of the nurses' station. There had to be some new rumor spreading through the hospital, because she noted that everyone was gathered around Kat, the queen of hospital gossip. Usually she would have paused to hear what the newest bit of gossip was, but today she didn't have time.

As soon as her paperwork was completed she changed out of her scrubs and headed back to her office. She didn't want to leave her patients waiting any longer. Irate pregnant women could be downright scary, and her staff could only appease them with promises of her return for so long.

John Lincoln, one of the pediatricians employed by the hospital working the obstetric hall, waved from the nursery hallway as she passed. A few seconds later she heard her name called and turned to find John was following her, with another man dressed in the hospital's light blue scrubs beside him.

Lana stopped and stared at the two men even as she shook her head in denial. There was no way this could be happening to her.

"Hey, Lana," John said as he approached. "This is Dr. Trent Montgomery. He's taken the *locum tenen* position we've had open since Dr. Lee left."

"We've met," Lana said as she turned toward Trent. "What are *you* doing here?"

"As John just told you, Ms. Sanders, I've accepted a temporary job with the pediatric department," Trent said. "I'm looking forward to the two of us working together."

Work with the person who was trying to take Maggie away from her? No way was *that* going to happen.

"But why? Why are you here?" Lana asked.

John looked at Lana, then back at Trent with a frown. "I take it you two know each other?" John asked.

"We've met." Lana said as she moved to one side of the hall to let a nurse pushing a patient in a wheelchair pass.

She noticed the look the nurse gave this new doctor in town. Yeah, she hated to admit it, but he was something to look at. Even with his high-dollar suit and cowboy boots gone he looked good. The pastel color of the cotton scrubs should have dimmed some of that masculine power that he threw off, but instead it seemed to amplify the hardness of the body they covered.

There would be a swarm of women circling around him as if he was roadkill as soon as they got a good look at him. And she would just leave them to it. Because no matter how good he looked she didn't want him anywhere near her and Maggie. Why was he doing this to her? Her life was stressful enough without him in *her* hospital, where she would be running into him all the time.

Crossing her arms, she leaned against the

wall. There was no way she was going to let him know how rattled he made her. She didn't care how sexy he looked standing there, she was going to let him know exactly how she felt about this ploy of his. Because that had to be what this was—just one more way to intimidate her into giving up Maggie.

But it wouldn't work, she was tougher than that. She would not let him get to her. There was too much at stake here. She had too much to lose to let a hard-bodied, hard-headed man get the best of her. She'd play his game if that was what it took to beat him.

"I'll catch up with you in the lounge," Trent said to John.

Lana waited till John was out of hearing range before asking the question that was burning her tongue. "What do you think you're doing here, Dr. Montgomery?" she asked. "Why aren't you back in Houston?"

Lana watched him take in her knowledge of that piece of information. Yeah, she'd done a little online stalking and it had paid off.

She'd found out that he worked in one of the largest women and children's hospitals in Houston as a pediatrician, for Pete's sake. Why he worked as a doctor at all, when he came from a family loaded with oil money, she didn't understand.

After seeing several pictures of him at different social affairs, all with a different beautiful woman on his arm, she had thought her heart would stop when she'd found an article that listed him as one of Houston's most eligible bachelors and had seen what was listed as his estimated net worth.

After that she had read everything the internet had on him, looking for something—anything—to use against him. But she hadn't found anything, and with every article her fear of losing Maggie had increased.

And apparently all the while she had been checking him out, he had been checking her out too. Because even if he had a good reason for leaving the hospital in Houston, the fact that he'd shown up at the hospital where she practiced out of all the hospitals in Miami meant he'd done his research. Or paid someone else to do it.

Wasn't that what the rich did? Hired someone else to do all the dirty work for them? There were no coincidences with men like Trent

Montgomery. No, he had an agenda in coming here, and she would find out what it was one way or the other.

"After my lawyer informed me that the courts would look favorably on me being within their district, I took leave from my job in Houston. Also, it made sense that it would be easier to work with you as far as visitation goes if I was living in the area. A temporary position opened up here, so I inquired and was offered the position."

As if the pediatric department was going to turn down a qualified pediatrician who had graduated from Emory and done a residency in neonatology when they were so short on staff.

"Besides, Miami is a beautiful city," he said as he moved closer, leaning in toward her as a group of staff members came down the hall. "Who *wouldn't* want to live here?"

She knew better than to let his look of innocence fool her, and she certainly wasn't going to let the fact that his body was now only inches away affect her.

"What did you tell the interviewers?" she continued, as she tried to ignore her speeding heartbeat. She hadn't discussed her court appearance with anyone at work—had just told those who'd asked that there had been a small delay in the paperwork at the court.

"I told them I had an interest in the position due to some business I had here in Miami," Trent said as he moved back a few inches. "I don't see why the hospital should have any concern for our private affairs."

Realizing she had been holding her breath, Lana let her lungs expand fully. The racing of her heart let her know she was allowing this man to get to her, and that wasn't acceptable. She would have to stop letting him intimidate her.

"And I'm supposed to believe that you just happened to end up at the same hospital where I work?"

Trent shrugged a shoulder, then gave her a smile that set her teeth on edge. This was a man who not only knew he was charming, but also knew how to use it to his advantage.

"That's what I thought," Lana said as she moved once more to let one of the unit nurses pass.

The fact that it was the same brunette nurse who had walked by earlier didn't surprise her.

Word had clearly already gotten out that there was a new male doctor on the unit, and the fact that he was sexy as hell meant that he would be getting even more attention than usual.

Soon the fact that she knew the new doc would come to the attention of the staff. And that was something that she didn't want to deal with right now.

Trent watched Lana as she stomped off, then stopped to pull a ringing phone from her pocket and answer it. He'd known she'd be angry when she found out he'd obtained a job at the hospital she worked at, and he couldn't blame her. What had surprised him was his reaction to her anger. The woman was as feisty as a wild filly, and reluctantly he had to admit that he'd found it entertaining and even a little arousing to watch her spit and sputter as she reached her boiling point with him.

And that was the strangest thing. Normally the sight of a woman's anger sent him running in the opposite direction. He'd seen enough of his mother's tantrums with his father to know he didn't want any part of that in his life. But this woman's anger was different. It was hot and furious, but at the same time it was controlled and non-threatening.

And she was sure something to see when her green eyes started to spark lightning strikes at him.

The woman would have his head if she knew that while she'd been doing all that ranting and raving he'd been thinking about how cute she was, trying to intimidate him with her five and a half feet against his six-feet-two-inch self.

The insistent screech of the beeper attached to his scrub bottoms went off and he read a message from the ER, concerning a preterm imminent delivery coming in.

"Which way to the ER?" he asked Lana as she ended her call.

For a second she just stared at him. Then, shaking her head, she turned down another hallway. "Come on, I'll show you," she said, not looking back to see if he was following her.

"There's a thirty-three-week antepartum coming in by ambulance," he said when he caught up with her.

"She's thirty-four weeks and six days. That was her husband on the phone," she said.

He knew those six days could make a big difference in the outcome of the delivery.

"Your patient?" he asked as they boarded an empty elevator to the bottom floor.

"Her name is Taylor. Her husband Dean says that her water suddenly broke and contractions started immediately. She has a history of preterm delivery and was on bedrest."

"How early were her other deliveries?"

"She's only had one. Her son Phillip was born at thirty-six weeks."

Trent waited for Lana to leave the elevator, then followed her through the double doors leading into the emergency room. Multiple glass-doored rooms opened up from what looked like the hub of the department, where nurses and doctors could be seen in front of monitors and answering phones.

"This way," Lana said as she turned left. "The department is basically set up with the trauma rooms on this end and the less urgent patients on the other."

She stopped in front of a large monitor set up at the end of the hallway then preceded into a room labeled Trauma Four.

As he entered the large room he noted the

baby-warming unit set up in the corner, and the nurses around them opening up the delivery set on a stand near an empty stretcher.

He grabbed Lana's arm and moved her back as a couple of emergency responders pushed a stretcher into the room, holding a pregnant woman panting and gripping the hands of the female responder.

As he gowned and gloved up he listened as the other responder gave his report to the room. "Spontaneous rupture of membranes twenty minutes ago with contractions starting immediately. Contractions now every two minutes. Vital signs with blood pressure elevated and heart-rate tachy at one-twenty."

He watched as Lana, also gowned and gloved, helped move the patient to the trauma bed then immediately did a vaginal exam, all the time talking to her patient in a calm voice.

"Is there time to move her upstairs?" he asked. He knew everyone would feel better if they could do the delivery on the obstetric unit.

"Nope," Lana said. "This one is coming right now."

A young nurse he was sure he had been introduced to earlier as belonging to the NICU team laid a blanket over his arms and he moved over to where Lana stood.

A breath later and Lana was holding out a small baby for the sobbing mother to see, then reaching for clamps and scissors as she made fast work of freeing the baby from its cord.

Rubbing its back to stimulate a cry, she turned toward him. Pausing for a second, she gave him an assessing look, then with a hesitant nod she handed the baby girl to him.

He took over from where Lana had stopped, and rubbed the baby's back as he did his assessment. A small cry started as he reached the warmer, and had turned into a howl by the time he laid her down.

The whole room broke out in cheers. He looked back to where Lana was comforting the new mom and saw big smiles on both their faces.

"Sounds like she has a good set of lungs to me," he said.

He waited for the nurses to bundle her up, then brought the squalling baby to its mother and introduced himself.

"She's a little early, so I'd like to take her up

to the nursery to observe her a little closer, but I'll get her back to you as soon as possible."

"But she's going to be okay?" the new mother asked.

"Her color looks good…she's going to get a seven and an eight on her Apgar. She was a bit slow starting up, but she's got the hang of it now, I'd say."

"As soon as you're ready I'll take you up to her," Lana told Taylor.

Trent laid the baby in the transport crib—she had calmed down some once she had been swaddled into a striped pink blanket—and followed the assigned nurse up to the nursery.

Considering everything that might have happened, he and Lana had managed to keep their personal issues out their jobs, thought Trent. He'd consider that a win for now.

He had no explanation for the way he responded to this woman. Since their first meeting thoughts of her had filled his mind, along with a deep pang of guilt at being the one who would to separate her from the little girl he could see she loved very much. But his agenda was set and nothing could change it now. He'd take care of his niece, just as his brother had asked him to, and he'd find a way to work with this midwife without everything around them exploding, while at the same time using the opportunity to find out everything he might be able to use in the custody battle.

He had to stop this adoption from going through. He wouldn't let his father ruin his niece's life the way he had ruined his brother's and mother's. He would protect her from his father no matter what it took, and once he had custody of his niece his brother's will would make sure his old man never had the power to hurt anyone again.

Lana took her place at Ms. Nelson's desk and waited for the social worker to finish her phone call. For once she had made it early for an appointment, and she planned on taking advantage of the time she had before Trent arrived.

Why the social worker felt it necessary for the two of them to meet together with her she didn't understand. The man rubbed her the wrong way, and she had spent the last few days doing her best to avoid him at the hospital, but there had been no way to get out of this meeting.

She would have to keep control of her temper, no matter how hard it was to stay in control when Trent Montgomery was in the room. Making a good impression with the social worker was too important. And, while her lawyer had given her his opinion of Trent's case for custody, she knew that a lot of the custody decision would be based on the social worker's investigation.

"Sorry about that, Lana," said Karen Nelson as she hung up the phone. "It's been a busy day today. I know this might sound cold, with your situation, but I just wish every child had two adults like you and Mr. Montgomery wanting them."

"That bad?" Lana asked.

She knew that there were a lot of children in foster homes who would never be adopted. She had seen it in her practice as a midwife, when one of her patients might give birth to a child she couldn't take care of and the child would go into the system. Then the mother wouldn't agree to give up her rights to the child, making it impossible for the child to be adopted, so they just continued to stay in the foster system year after year.

Thankfully Chloe had made it clear in her notarized letter, and later in her correspondence with the court, that she wanted Maggie to be adopted. If only more mothers like her could see that they wouldn't be letting their children down but instead opening up a better option for them.

"Yeah," the social worker said as she finger-combed the back of her hair, took a deep breath and then seemed to reset herself back into work mode as she started going through the files on her desk.

Not for the first time Lana wondered why someone would ever go into social work—especially in Children and Families. The pressure to ensure the safety of all the children they were responsible for must be mind-boggling.

"While we wait for Dr. Montgomery to arrive let's talk about how *you're* doing. I know this isn't easy for you. Are you hanging in there okay?"

"I know you're right about Maggie being a lucky little girl. I get that," Lana said, "but how much harm will come to her if she's taken away from the only home she's ever known and placed with a stranger? She's been through so much already."

"I'm her uncle—not a stranger. And surely you can see the advantages of a child being raised among her biological family?" Trent said as he stared down at Lana.

"She's not even two. She's not really interested in your stock portfolio," Lana said.

How had she let him sneak up on her like that?

"Dr. Montgomery—" the social worker started.

"Ma'am," Trent said as he tipped his big cowboy hat before sitting down beside her. "Please, call me Trent."

Lana watched as he gave the woman what she had overheard one of the nurses call his "killer" smile. He was such a suck-up.

"Trent, please take a seat."

The social worker's smile beamed back at Trent, causing Lana to knot her hands into fists in her lap when what she really wanted to do was wrap them around the man's neck.

"I was just telling Lana that I know this is not easy for her. It must be hard for you too, having just lost your brother and now moving to Miami on such short notice. I was surprised when your lawyer notified me that you were relocating temporarily. I'm sure this has disrupted your life. You must have been very close to your brother to be willing to make these changes."

Lana saw the smile on his face tighten. She didn't have any doubt that there was a story there. Had there been trouble between the brothers? Was there something she could use?

"With my brother gone, I feel that it is my responsibility to make sure his daughter is taken care of," Trent said, and then he turned in his chair toward Lana. "That's what families are for. Wouldn't you agree, Lana?"

Lana looked into Trent's eyes. Somehow he had managed to turn the tables on her, making any protest she might come up with seem heartless and uncaring. Well, two could play that game.

"Yes, families *are* important. That's why I've decided to agree to you spending some time with Maggie," Lana said, and she watched Trent to see his reaction to this piece of news.

She'd thought her lawyer crazy when he'd advised her to consider the visitation, but after he had explained that it would be a way to show the courts that she was willing to allow Maggie to see her biological family after the adoption it had made sense. She was willing to do whatever was necessary to keep her little girl—even if it meant spending time with an irritating cowboy.

"That sounds great, Lana. I'm so glad that the two of you are working together so well," Ms. Nelson said. "The reason I asked for this meeting was so that we could discuss where we go from here. I know the two of you are on different sides in this case, but I want you both to remember the most important thing to consider here is Maggie and her wellbeing."

"Of course," Lana said, and then looked over at Trent.

"Certainly, Ms. Nelson," Trent said.

Lana watched the corners of Trent's mouth twitch, as if trying to hold back a smile. Why did she suddenly feel she had fallen into a trap? A trap with a big, bad smiling wolf in it, waiting to devour her.

"Good," said Ms. Nelson. "I take it you two will come to terms with the visitation arrangements, so unless there is anything else that comes up I won't need to see either of you again till the DNA test results come back."

"That's fine," Trent said. "I feel sure me and Lana will be able to come to an agreement."

"I'm sure we will," Lana said. *An agreement?* She'd have to remind him that she would be the person in control of their meetings.

"Thank you for your time, Ms. Nelson," Trent said, blessing the social worker with another one of his smiles as they rose to leave.

Lana walked beside Trent as they left the office building. He'd been quiet as they had ridden down on an overcrowded elevator. It had been uncomfortable, being squeezed next to him. It seemed that no matter how much she tried, she couldn't get away from the man.

They could play nice together in front of the social worker, but that was as far as she could go with it. Just standing next to him was enough to fire up her defenses. This man was a threat to her and she knew she had to stay alert.

Of course there was that saying about keeping your enemies closer than your friends. Was that what Trent was doing by coming to work where he knew he'd be able to observe her? Not that there was any dirt he could dig up on her. She had never lived much of an exciting life.

She had even started to think lately that she was getting to be just plain old boring.

Maybe after Maggie's adoption had taken place she'd take up a hobby, or get back in the dating pool. *Maybe.*

Thoughts of Joe and the way their relationship had ended left her shaking her head. Even though the man had professed that he loved her, it hadn't been enough. Not enough to make him want a future with a woman who couldn't give him children.

Her dream of a forever marriage—a marriage filled with love and support like her parents'—had been destroyed the day they'd broken up and she'd had to accept that she would probably never be able to find a man who would accept her as she was, damaged and broken.

No, she wasn't going anywhere near heartache any time soon. She had created her own little family with Maggie and that was enough. Now she just had to find a way to keep her family intact and get this cowboy back to Texas. And, as much as it was going to kill her, it was going to mean spending some time with him.

"Look, we need to talk about this visitation.

There will have to be some rules. Are you hungry?" Lana asked.

"Yeah, I skipped lunch so that I could get off on time," Trent said.

"There's a little Cuban deli I usually stop by when I'm down here," Lana said. "The food's good and the people are friendly."

Lana watched as Trent's lips twitched, as if he was unable to decide how to take her invitation, and then they parted. Something about his bright smile caused her warning bells to go off. *Danger, danger*, they said, but it was too late. For the second time that day she felt as if she was the fly that was getting caught up in Trent's web.

Maybe from now on they should discuss these visitations over the phone.

"Sounds good," Trent said. "Do we walk or drive?"

"Walk," Lana said.

She found herself about to smile back at him before she caught herself. She couldn't let herself be influenced by this man's charms. They would discuss the necessary arrangements and maybe she'd also try to pry a little information out of him. This was about Maggie—not the stupid way his smile made her legs wobble as she started walking up the street.

She had found Café MaRita on one of her visits to the Children and Families Department office, and she was glad to see the two sisters who owned the deli were working when she arrived at the walk-up window.

"Hey, Rita," Lana said, then waved to Mary in the back, where she was putting together the spicy sandwiches they were known for. "Can I get two Cubanos, an iced tea and…?" Lana turned to Trent questioning.

"A coffee, please," Trent said. "A *cafecito*?"

The small Cuban woman smiled at his pronunciation of the word for a coffee topped with sugary foam.

"I like this one," Rita said, and she winked at Trent. "He's dark and hot. Like my coffee. If you decide to get rid of him let me know."

"Oh, no," Lana said as she felt heat spread up her face, "it's not like that—"

"I'll make it a point to look you up when she's finished with me," Trent said, interrupting Lana.

Did the man have to flirt with every woman he met? Taking the sandwiches, she found an empty picnic table set out in the front of the deli and started dividing the food while she waited for Trent.

Watching him as he talked to the older Cuban woman while she prepared their drinks, Lana was impressed at how at ease he seemed with people. He had the ability to charm everyone he met—well, everyone except for her. The only thing *she* would find charming about him would be his backside headed out of town.

Trent watched Lana as she bit into her sandwich. He could see she was concentrating on something, and he didn't think it was just the sandwich she was eating—though she did seem to be enjoying it. It was nice to see a woman eat her food without any posturing about diets and calories.

He watched as the pink tip of her tongue slipped out and caught some of the juice running down the side of her mouth. From nowhere a burst of desire filled him, and he felt a jolt of arousal as it spread down his groin. Another swipe of her tongue along the crease of her mouth had his pants becoming uncomfortably tight.

He shifted in his seat, causing Lana to suddenly look up from her meal, and he knew the second their eyes connected that he wasn't hiding the hunger that had hit him. The surprise came when her eyes changed and she lifted her eyebrows, silently questioning him. If this was any other woman he might have thought she was purposely playing with him, but that just didn't seem like Lana's style.

"Sorry, I haven't found a way to eat these without making a mess," Lana said.

"That's okay. I'm actually enjoying watching you." Trent said, then watched spots of color flush her cheeks.

"Tell me why you decided to go into medicine instead of staying in the family business," Lana said, changing the subject.

His gut tightened as he thought of the decision he had made to follow his dreams. Would his brother still be here if he hadn't left him behind with his father? He had let Michael down when he'd walked away from his father's expectations for him. In saving himself from becoming the heir apparent to the Montgomery empire he had left his brother to deal with their father's unreasonable demands and bouts of temper.

No one had ever been good enough for their father. No one had been able to stand up to the old man's expectations. Not him, not their mother, and certainly not his brother. He had urged his brother to follow after him and get away from his father's influence, but Michael hadn't been strong enough. He'd even tried to talk his brother into the two of them joining together and using their share of the company stocks to oust their father from his position as head of the company, but Michael had refused.

Instead, Michael had continually tried to earn their father's approval, and when that hadn't happened he had turned to the same thing their mother had used to escape their father: alcohol. And when that hadn't been enough he had turned to drugs, until finally the two had killed him.

"You could say I did follow in one of my family's footsteps. My Uncle Jim was a surgeon. He had a lot of influence on my decision," Trent answered. She didn't need to know the turmoil his decision had caused to his family.

"Any regrets?" Lana asked.

"What?" Trent asked, startled by the question. Did she know about the division in his family? Had she somehow learned about the threats and bribes his father constantly sent him, trying to get him to come back to the family-run business?

"I don't know much about the oil business, but I do know about all the demands and sacrifices a medical career requires. It just seems you could have had a pretty good thing going for you, working in your own company," Lana said.

"I find being a pediatrician very satisfying and challenging. And I can make far more of a difference as a pediatrician than as a businessman, don't you think?" Trent said.

He stood and started gathering up items from the table to throw out. For now, the less this woman knew about his business, the better.

"You said you wanted to discuss the visitations?" Trent said.

"Yes, I do. I hope you understand that just because I'm letting you spend time with Maggie it doesn't mean I've changed my mind about keeping her?"

"I think you've made that plain," Trent said.

The only way she could have made her intentions any plainer would have been for her to tattoo them on her body. He had no doubt this woman was going to fight him all the way.

"Okay, then. I'm willing to allow visitations as long as it's understood that I'm in charge of everything that concerns her. I'll always be present and I'll have the final word on when and where."

After the short walk back, Trent watched as Lana's car pulled out of the parking garage. Nothing he had learned so far, today or at the hospital, indicated that she was anything other than a young woman working as a midwife and raising a child she loved as her own. He couldn't help but like her, and he hated that she was being pulled into this mess with his father, but he didn't see any way out of it. And it was better that she had to deal with him instead of the old man. At least he fought fair. He couldn't say that about his father.

They had arranged a time for him to visit Maggie during their walk back to their cars and Lana had been more than fair with him. Everything he had heard around the hospital about Lana had been positive. He even felt a little guilty that he had taken a job here to see what he could dig up on her. From what he had seen so far there wasn't anything in her character that made him think he needed to be worried about his niece not being cared for, or that there was anything he could use against her in the court case.

But he knew how appearances could be deceptive. Hadn't his mom had everyone fooled until it was too late? No one had ever known about the fights between his parents. or the times when his mother had never even got out of the bed in the mornings, leaving two little boys to care for themselves.

He knew first-hand that no one ever really knew what went on behind the closed doors of a home. No matter how much Lana Sanders looked like the perfect mother, he would be sticking to the woman like glue until he had custody of his niece and knew without a doubt that she was safe.

CHAPTER THREE

TRENT STOOD ON the sidewalk outside Lana's home. He had seen a lot of these small block houses since he had arrived in Miami and though they were older buildings, he liked them.

The neat bungalows reminded him of the difference between his life in Houston and Maggie and Lana's here. While his condo in the busy metropolis area was modern, with all the amenities available, Lana's front yard was full of pink and yellow blooms and looked friendly and inviting. And whereas a doorman met visitors on arrival in his building, a colorful gnome sat on Lana's small porch, holding a "Welcome" sign which made even Trent feel as if he would be greeted warmly.

Of course neither of the two places compared to his father's ranch, where he had grown up. Even with the chaos that had made up his parents' relationship he had always felt at home there, with its sprawling acres of pastures. He had been able to escape for long rides on one of his horses and he'd come back feeling better every time. He had to admit he missed that feeling of being at home, of belonging somewhere.

Lana answered the door looking every bit the suburban mom in her tee shirt and jeans. While he might have thought the "mom look" would put him off, he was surprised to find that he liked it on her. She looked comfortable in the mommy role.

"Hey," Lana said as she held the door open.

There was a nervousness about her today that had him thinking she was having second thoughts about letting him into her home.

"Is everything okay?" Trent asked. "If you've changed you mind and want to...?"

"No," Lana said. "I'm sorry. Come in. Maggie's in her room, playing."

Lana directed Trent down the hall, where he found a room decorated in light pinks and purples. Sitting in the middle of the floor was a little girl, pouring what had to be pretend tea into a group of small cups. The table where she sat was surrounded by tiny chairs, upon one of which a rabbit was waiting to be served.

"Maggie?" Lana called the toddler's attention to her. "This is the man I told you was coming to see you. His name is Trent."

The raven-haired child looked up at Trent and a long-forgotten memory hit him as if it were a physical blow. While Maggie's eyes were blue, like both his and his brother's, the shade was slightly different. He had only seen that shade of clear cerulean blue once and, though his memories of his mother after all these years were few, he could still remember her eyes. The same eyes that now stared back at him from the face of the small girl who was studying him with a seriousness he was surprised to see in one so young.

"Maggie, will you let Trent play with you while I get your snack?" Lana asked.

"Cookie?" the child said as she looked back at her.

Trent watched as the toddler turned her smile on Lana. It was easy to see that Maggie had already begun developing the Montgomery negotiation skills.

"You can have two," Lana said as she held up two fingers, "with your juice."

Maggie smiled back at Lana, then got up and walked over to him. "Play?" she asked as she looked up at him.

"Ah…okay…" Trent said, surprised by the nervousness that suddenly hit him.

He was a pediatrician, for heaven's sake. He cared for kids of all ages in his practice. There was no reason for this one little girl to scare him, but inside his heart he knew there *was* a difference between this child and his patients. This was his brother's little girl. She was *family.*

Before the panic had time to overwhelm him, the child said something in an unknown language, then pulled on his hand. He shot a look back at Lana, who just smiled at them, then turned and left the room.

Lana stood and looked out the kitchen window. She couldn't help the smile she saw reflected in the window pane. The look on Trent's face had been priceless. How could a man who took care of sick children every day at work be scared of one little girl?

Just knowing that he was as uneasy about this

meeting as she was made her feel a little better. She had been nervous about having Trent in her home. She knew her home was old and small, but she had made a comfortable place there for herself and Maggie. Would a man like Trent be able to appreciate the small house for what it was? A home where she and Maggie had become a family?

She watched as the smile that had been reflected just moments earlier disappeared.

A family—everything a little girl dreamed of. But when you were fifteen years old, and adults were telling you that you had cancer, the last thing you thought of was your infertility. She had just wanted to know if she would live long enough to make it to junior prom. But while she had worried about the chemo and the radiation causing her hair to fall out, she should have been worried about what the treatments were doing to the inside of her body instead.

Being told that you would not be able to have children at any age was a horrible thing. Being a teenager and learning that you would never be able to give birth to a child had been devastating.

She had given up on her dream of having a

family and instead had thrown herself into high school and later her college education. Once she had gotten her degree in nursing she had found her calling in labor and delivery. If she could not have a child herself, at least she could help bring children into the world.

Then during her last year at midwifery school her Prince Charming had come and she had thought her life would be perfect from then on out. When a year later she had discovered that her prince, Joe, was really a frog, warts and all, it had been too late.

When the man she'd loved had told her that he just couldn't settle for a woman who wasn't able to give him children she had hit the lowest point in her life. But then Maggie had come along and everything had felt right. She *knew* she was meant to have Maggie, but how could she convince the man in the next room?

She finished fixing the drinks—two iced teas for them and one sippy cup of juice for Maggie—and then stacked some of the cookies she had made earlier that morning on a tray. She stopped at the door, then covered her mouth to hold a laugh inside as she watched her daughter initiate Trent the manly cowboy into the world of playing pretend with a little girl.

He sat on the floor cross-legged, in front of the small table, with a pink polka dot hat on top of his head, and pretended to drink from a small plastic cup.

"Would you like some real tea?" Lana asked. "Sorry, I don't have any coffee."

"Tea's fine," Trent said. "But it will have to be some brew to compete with Maggie's. Isn't that right, Maggie?"

Maggie gave Trent a beaming smile. Somehow in the few minutes Lana had been gone Trent had managed to charm her little girl—not that she could blame her. There wasn't a female around who could withstand this man when he was smiling like he was right then.

She had heard all the rumors about the hospital nurses making fools of themselves around him, and if she was honest with herself she had to admit that being around him made her feel just as enchanted as the rest of womankind.

That was just what the man *wanted* her to feel, but she wasn't stupid enough to let a little bit of physical attraction muddle her brain. If he thought that he could charm her into letting her guard down around him, he was wrong.

Getting Maggie to settle down for a nap after finishing her snack had been a chore, but finally the toddler had tearfully waved goodbye to Trent and Lana had carried the worn-out baby to her room and put her in her crib.

She shut the door quietly and found Trent standing behind her.

"She's beautiful," Trent said, with a reverence that touched something deep down inside her.

Lana felt the same way every day she spent with Maggie. She was surprised at how sharing this feeling of caring for a child made her suddenly feel so close to him. Was this another ploy on his part?

"Thanks for letting me see her," Trent said softly.

Lana pushed her hair out of her face and looked up at him. It was easy to see that he had been moved by the time he had spent with Maggie. It had to be hard for him after the loss of his brother—to see this reminder of him.

"Are you okay?" she asked.

"It shouldn't be me standing here," he said. "It should be my brother."

"What happened to him, Trent?"

"Michael had the same problems as Chloe. His addiction of choice was alcohol, though recently he had begun combining it with drugs. One night he just took too many…"

Michael's voice cracked for a second, and then he cleared his throat.

"And now he's not here to enjoy that beautiful little girl," he said.

Suddenly she was aware of the closeness caused by the small hallway, and for a moment she felt the need to reach out and touch him, to smooth away the pain she saw in his face. And then she remembered the reason he was standing here in her house. He had come to establish a relationship with her daughter—a relationship that he intended to continue by taking Maggie away from her.

"I won't let you take her without a fight," Lana said.

Her body was relaxed, more comfortable with the anger inside her than with the attraction that had wound so tightly inside her body just seconds earlier.

"I know," Trent said.

His whisper seemed to bounce off the walls of the hallway. He reached up and pushed a stray hair behind her ear, his touch leaving a soft tingle behind. Then he turned and walked out of her house, leaving her alone with her young daughter, and for the first time since she had moved in it felt empty.

She'd worked hard to make her home a safe place, her retreat from the world after a hard day. She had accepted that she might never meet a man who could give her the forever love that she longed for—the type of love she'd witnessed between her parents—but she had made a home here for her little family and she would not let anyone take that away from her.

"You are doing *great*, Jaden," Lana said as she watched her patient breathe through another contraction.

The fetal heart tones were reassuring, but the labor process had slowed down. If there wasn't a change soon, the OB on call would start questioning if Jaden was going to be able to have a vaginal birth. The baby's posterior position was just not allowing it to come farther down into the birth canal.

"We can try moving you back onto your knees and see if we can get the baby to turn, if you'd like," Lana said.

"It didn't help last time," Jaden said as she took a deep breath and prepared for the next contraction.

"I know you wanted to do this without any type of pain control—" Lana started.

"She went through all the classes," Jaden's sister said.

"I know, and she's doing great. But the labor has gotten long now, and I really think we need to consider all our options. That includes an epidural," Lana said as she took the cool wash-cloth a nurse handed her and wiped Jaden's face.

"They said it would slow down labor," Jaden said.

"Sometimes it can, but right now your labor is not progressing at all," Lana said.

"I'll think about it," Jaden said.

The phone clipped to Lana's green scrubs pocket vibrated. She knew it had to be the of-fice again.

"I'm going to step out for a moment," Lana said. "Why don't you think about whether getting an epidural is something you want to do while I take this call?"

Lana nodded to the nurse and walked out of the room. A call to her office told her that the department was packed with patients waiting to see her. The crowd was getting restless and her staff needed to know what to tell the women who were waiting.

Some days Lana needed to be cloned. Today was one of those days.

After talking with her office nurse, and catching up on Jaden's progress notes, she returned to the labor room. The sight of the anesthesiologist standing at the bottom of the bed and talking to her patient told her Jaden had decided to opt for the epidural.

"They decided on the epidural," the nurse, Shelley, whispered as she leaned toward Lana.

The door opened and Trent walked in, carrying a clipboard. He nodded to her, then moved over to Jaden as the anesthesiologist started setting up his tray.

"Trent is so good with the patients," the nurse

said. "He makes a point to come and see them before they deliver, and they love him."

"His name is Dr. Montgomery," Lana said, and then regretted it as soon as she saw the questioning look on Shelley's face.

It wasn't any of her business if Trent got friendly with the nurses. She couldn't even blame them for wanting to get his attention. The man appeared to be a sexual magnet for women. Didn't she know it herself? She couldn't keep her own traitorous body from responding to the sexual pull of him, but that didn't mean she had to like it.

She moved over to the bed and helped the nurse position Jaden for her epidural. Trent stood to one side while she answered some of Jaden's sister's questions.

She thought about that moment in her hallway, when for a second she had felt a connection with him, When he'd touched her she had been sure he had felt it too. Had that moment been real or had she just imagined it? And why was she standing in the middle of a labor room thinking about Trent instead of her patient?

Forcing her attention back to where it should have stayed, Lana took her place to help her patient concentrate on her breathing and remain in the proper position. Just as they were ready, her phone rang.

"If you need to get that I can help," Trent said. "Unless you want to?" He addressed the patient's sister.

"Oh, no, I hate needles," the sister said, and she moved across the room as far away as she could.

As her phone went to voicemail Lana relaxed. Then it immediately rang again. Someone was certainly being persistent.

"Have you ever helped with an epidural before?" she asked.

"I can't say I have, but I'm willing to learn," Trent said.

"Okay, come over here and help support her," Lana said as her phone continued to ring.

She traded places with Trent, then left the room to take the call.

When she stepped back into the room she was hit with a picture of Trent bent over Jaden, talking quietly as he assured her that they were almost finished. Anyone else walking in might easily have thought he was just another father helping his wife get through her labor.

The thought caused a small pain in her heart.

Fifteen minutes later Jaden was lying down and tilted onto her left side. While it would take several minutes for the medication to reach its full effect, Lana could tell by the way Jaden was starting to relax into the bed that she was already starting to feel some relief.

Lana checked the fetal monitor, then suggested a nap for both Jaden and her sister.

"Since you seem to always be feeding me, I thought I'd buy you lunch this time," Trent said as they stepped out of the labor room.

Lana glanced down the hallway and saw that two of the labor nurses had stopped and were looking their way. While she and Trent were standing outside one of the hospital rooms it would look as if they were discussing a patient's care, and no one would make any comments. But if they were sitting together at a table in the hospital café…?

That would definitely stir up the rumor mill.

"It might not be a good idea," Lana said.

"I promise I won't discuss the court case," Trent said, and then leaned against the wall looking at her expectantly. "I heard they're serving fried potato casserole today. You wouldn't want to miss *that*, would you?"

"So I treat you to the city's best *cubano* and my famous chocolate chip cookies and the best you can do is that? Besides, I need to get back to my office."

"I'd be happy to do better," Trent said. "How about dinner Saturday night?"

Lana felt her senses go on alert. The teasing tone in his voice was gone now. Was this another one of his tricks to get to her?

"I thought we had agreed to a visitation with Maggie on Saturday at the beach?" Lana asked.

"I'm talking about after our day at the beach," Trent said.

Lana watched as Trent pushed off the wall and took a step closer. That flirty smile he had flashed earlier was gone, leaving her in no doubt that he was serious in his invitation.

"What do you want from me?" she asked, unable to keep the stress from her voice.

Was this another ploy to get her to cave in to the Montgomery demands for custody of Maggie?

"Look, Lana, whether we like it or not, until the court makes its decision we're going to have to get along. It just seems like it would be easier if we got to know each other better."

And then his smile was back with all its magical appeal.

"I'm really not a bad guy, you know."

Maybe he wasn't a bad guy, but he was still the enemy.

"Okay," Lana said.

If he wanted to get to know her better—fine. It wasn't as if that was going to change her mind about keeping Maggie. Besides, maybe if he got to know her better he'd see that Maggie was where she needed to be. It would definitely be harder for him to take her daughter away from someone he'd come to know instead of a stranger.

It was a long shot, but she would take any chances she could get to keep her daughter.

"But don't say I didn't warn you about the fried potato casserole. You'll need to get your cholesterol checked as soon as lunch is over."

She arrived back on the labor and delivery unit to find Jaden almost ready for delivery. After less than an hour of pushing she delivered a healthy eight-pound baby boy. As Trent handed the new mom her baby her patient thanked him for all his help, and as Lana left the unit she thought about how Trent had been so good with her.

The quick lunch they had shared had been relaxing. They had discussed some of the differences between his job on the pediatric floor at his Houston hospital and the neonatal unit he was working in here. She'd been able to tell he had a true love for his job in Houston, and she couldn't help but wonder again at his choice to leave it to pursue his court case.

Neither one of them had brought up the custody case, and for the first time there hadn't been any conflict between them. Was it possible that they could work together without letting their outside problems get in the way? It looked as if they might be able to, but she knew she was walking on thin ice when it came to any type of relationship between the two of them.

It would be a very easy man to let her guard down around a man like Trent, and no matter how at ease she might feel around him she needed to remember they were on opposite sides when it came to Maggie. That was truly all that counted.

CHAPTER FOUR

AS SHE DRAGGED HERSELF through the front door, the quiet house told Lana that Amanda had already put Maggie to bed. She hated to miss that time of day, when Maggie, with damp curls and smelling of baby wash, would climb up into her lap and snuggle while they read a book together, but as hard as she'd tried she hadn't been able to catch up at the office without staying late.

As soon as she shut the door Amanda stepped out of the kitchen carrying two glasses of some kind of pink fruity-looking drink.

"Energy smoothie," she said as she handed one of the drinks to Lana. "You sounded like you could use a pick-me-up when you called."

"Thanks," Lana said.

The refreshing liquid slid down easily, bringing a soothing feeling through her body. She took a quick peek into Maggie's room and found her sleeping like an angel, then headed back into the living room. She let herself slump down on her couch and found herself relaxing for the first time all day.

She toed her shoes off and wiggled her tired feet. Dorothy in *The Wizard of Oz* was so right. There was no place like home.

"I left some pasta on the stove. You want me to fix you a plate?" Amanda asked.

"No, thanks. I'll get it later."

"Bad day, huh?" the young woman asked.

Amanda had been Maggie's live-in babysitter since Maggie was two months old. She had been there on those days when Lana had come home thrilled with the experience of having been a part of bringing a new baby into the world, and she had been there when Lana had come home emotionally torn up after giving an expectant mom news that had destroyed their hopes and dreams.

Today had been neither of those. It had just been very long.

She played over the events of the day, remembering the delivery she had done and the part Trent had played in it.

She hadn't been able to get his invitation to dinner off her mind. She would have to decide what she wanted to do about it. It should be an easy decision. She had told herself not to let their relationship become any more personal, but after their lunch together she was finding it hard to ignore her desire to see him some more.

"Lana…?"

"Oh, sorry. I zoned out for a minute," she answered. "Not really bad. I just ran late all day after a long delivery."

She sipped her drink and considered her options. She could try to ignore Trent, with the hope that he would soon go away, or she could let him get to know her better, with the hope that she would make him see that she was the perfect mother for Maggie.

The question of why he was pushing to spend more time with her kept circling in her mind, reminding her to beware of good-looking men with possible hidden agendas…reminding her of the need to stay on alert. What was he up to?

"What do you think about Trent Montgomery?" she asked.

Amanda studied her over the rim of her glass, then finally asked, "As an uncle to Maggie?"

"No. Not in relationship to Maggie."

Lana sat up straight and adjusted the pillows

on the couch. Grabbing one, she hugged it close to her body, then combed her fingers through the satin cord tassels.

"So you mean as a man?" Amanda asked.

Lana nodded at Amanda. While she knew the babysitter was very protective of both her and Maggie, she also knew that she'd be honest and fair in her opinion.

"Well…" A big smile spread across Amanda's face. "If it wasn't for his involvement in stopping the adoption, I'd probably be thinking about jumping his bones—just like you."

"Amanda!" she said, feigning shock and throwing the pillow she'd been holding at her friend's laughing face. "I haven't—"

"Well, maybe you should." Amanda laughed again as Lana grabbed another pillow and shot it toward her.

She could feel the heat of embarrassment spreading up her face. Okay, maybe since they'd had that moment in her hallway she *had* been having dreams which included getting Trent out of his scrubs. Or his suit. Or whatever he had been wearing the last time she saw him. But she wasn't going to admit it.

"He asked me out."

"Like on a date?"

"More of a let's-get-to-know-each-other-better kind of thing, I think," Lana said.

"Wow," Amanda said. "Are you going?"

"I'm thinking about it," she answered.

The look of surprise on Amanda's face mirrored her own. Was she seriously thinking about spending time alone with Trent? Was she crazy?

"I don't know if I should be more shocked by the fact that you're even considering going out or by who you're considering going out *with*," Amanda said.

"Trent wants Maggie, Amanda—nothing else."

"What about you? What do *you* want?" Amanda asked.

And that was the problem. One moment the man was irritating her, with his *I'm Maggie's uncle and I know what's best for her* attitude, and the next he was charming her with that Texas drawl and that sexy smile of his. And then there was that irritating tingling she felt whenever he was near—a physical awareness of him that made her want to run far away but at the same time want to seek him out.

None of it made sense, and spending more time with him would be like playing with fire. No matter how safe you thought you were, there was still a possibility that you'd get burnt.

Of course the good thing was that he'd be leaving as soon as the court came up with a ruling on Maggie's custody. A ruling that could result in her losing Maggie.

That thought sobered her out of her daydream. Making sure that didn't happen was what she needed to concentrate on. As soon as the adoption was finalized she would think about getting back out in the dating jungle. The attraction she was feeling for Trent was just another sign that she'd been too long without a man in her life. She'd thought after what she'd gone through with Joe that she had accepted she had no need for a man in her life. Apparently she had been wrong.

"I just want life to go back to the way it was before he showed up," Lana said. "But I need to keep an eye on him. Hopefully he'll be leaving soon."

"And without Maggie," Amanda said, with a confidence that Lana wished she felt.

"Without Maggie," Lana seconded, and the two of them clinked their glasses together.

As the bikini clad blond roller-skated around them Lana considered her choice of beach once again. While she was usually comfortable with her body, now, seeing all the perfectly tanned beauties who flocked to the South Beach location. she felt self-conscious, knowing her body was not like the thin, willowy specimens out on display today.

She had what her mother had always referred to as "a curvy figure." She had never been lacking in the breast department, and her hips and thighs were definitely wider than those belonging to the women on all the magazine covers that tried to tell you what you should look like.

Her body was basically just like the rest of her—nothing above average—and up until now she had always been okay with that. She knew the only reason she felt inadequate now was because she had seen the women Trent was normally photographed with. But she wasn't one of those women. She was just herself and she needed to accept it.

"Here?" Trent motioned toward the crosswalk over to the beach.

He had insisted on carrying Maggie through the crowd, instead of using the stroller she kept in the car to help with carrying both baby and all the items that were needed when traveling with a toddler.

"Let's wait till the next one," Lana said, not wanting to mention that she was trying to avoid the topless section of the beach.

"You know, we have beaches in Texas, but they're not nearly as entertaining as this," Trent said as a second barely clad woman skated past.

A sleek cherry-red muscle car drove by, blaring music out the windows, making it impossible to talk. It was still quite early for the weekend crowd, but it appeared they were all ready to party even at this hour.

Lana had chosen to go early so that she could get Maggie back home in time for a nap, but she was also hoping to escape before the afternoon crowd showed up, making it impossible to get through on the small streets crowded with shops and restaurants.

"We can take the next crossover."

Lana moved in close, trying to avoid a group

of tourists standing outside the old-fashioned soda shop. She felt the warm heat of Trent's hand when he reached around her waist and guided her through the crowd. They crossed the street to the entrance for the beach. When they reached the thick sand he moved his hand to grip her elbow, helping her as she plodded down to the shore.

They found a space with room to stretch out a blanket and Trent let the toddler down, but kept hold of her hand as she pulled him closer to the waves.

Grabbing some sunscreen, Lana joined them and began to slather lotion over Maggie as she giggled and stomped her feet in the water.

"Be still, you little wiggle-worm!" Lana laughed as she fought to make sure there weren't any areas not covered.

Maggie, deciding it was a game, squirmed around Trent's leg, causing Lana to miss the intended cheek and smear lotion across Trent's leg. At the feel of the coarse hair on this intimate part of Trent's thigh Lana's face flushed with redness. This had been such a bad idea.

"I'm so sorry…" Lana said, and she scooted back fast, almost tripping over Maggie.

"No problem—thanks for helping me with the sunscreen," Trent said.

She watched a smile curve across his lips that let her know he found her embarrassment amusing.

He picked up Maggie and held her out at arm's length. "I'll hold her for you."

Lana quickly finished with the lotion and then grabbed the little hand Maggie held out to her after Trent put her back down on the sand.

"Me play. *Now*," Maggie demanded, and she pulled down on both the adult hands holding her back from the waves.

They walked out a couple feet until Maggie could feel the cool water lap against her legs. Again she pulled down on Lana and Trent's arms, and she started swinging back and forth while dragging her feet through the water and giggling.

All around them people were wading out into the water or stretching out on the coarse sand. It was a great place for Maggie to play, and in minutes all three of them were laughing. with water soaking through their clothes.

They walked back to their blanket, where

Trent set Maggie up with her pail and shovel. Lana started to peel her wet shirt off, then turned just in time to see Trent lift his own shirt over his head. For a second she had a full view of a firm, toned chest with a small strip of hair. She followed the dark line down to where it disappeared into a water-soaked bathing suit that molded around his groin, leaving very little to her imagination.

Realizing she had been guilty of staring, she looked up to find Trent's eyes glued to her face. She had definitely been caught. Where was a Florida sink hole when you needed one?

She jerked her tee shirt up over her face and then peeked through the armhole to see him still staring at her. The stupidity of hiding there, with her shirt over her head, just increased her embarrassment. Acting like a sex-starved female was bad enough—not having the courage to own up to it was worse.

She finished pulling off her shirt, moving slowly to disguise her nervousness. One look at Trent had her wishing her shirt was back in place. A smile still filled his face, but the heat now in his eyes out-burned the Florida sun.

A warm stream of desire began in her chest and then flowed down to pool deep into her core. How did he *do* that? It was as if he was touching her with those beautiful eyes, melting her with the heat she saw in them. As if reading her mind, he swept her body with one more appreciative look, causing her body to respond with a need she had long forgotten and didn't want to remember.

"Me, me!" Maggie cried as she pulled down on Trent's bathing suit, not happy that she had lost her new friend's attention.

"What a beautiful child—you must be very proud."

The voice cut through her thoughts and Lana looked over to where an older couple had stopped to admire Maggie. She was used to being stopped by strangers, commenting on her little girl.

"Thank you," Lana said.

"It's so nice to see a young family spending time together," the elderly woman continued.

"Oh, we're not—" Lana started to correct her.

"You're a lucky man," the white-headed man complimented Trent.

"Yes, I am," Trent said as he placed his arm

around Lana's shoulders and pulled her close to his side. "Thank you."

The couple waved goodbye to Maggie, then continued their walk down the beach hand in hand.

"Okay. Let's make us a big castle," Trent said as he let go of Lana and knelt down to help fill the pail full of wet sand.

"Why did you do that?" Lana sputtered.

"Did you *really* want to try to explain our unique relationship to them?"

Unique? Yeah, that would be a good description for them.

No one seeing the two of them together with Maggie would think there was a battle going on between the two of them. For a minute while they had played together in the water she had forgotten herself. It had just seemed so natural and right for the two of them to be enjoying time with this beautiful child.

She knew she needed to take a step back from Trent and see what was really happening here. She had no doubt that there were ulterior motives behind all the attention he had been giving her lately.

Playing "Mommy and Daddy" with Trent

would only get her hurt. It was too close to the happily-ever-after dream she'd carried with her for years—the dream that had died when Joe had walked out on her.

She and Maggie made a great family. They didn't need anyone else in their life.

"I think I'll stretch out and catch some sun, if you don't mind watching her," Lana said as she stepped away.

"Sure. Relax. I've got Maggie," he said as he looked across at her.

Knowing he hadn't meant that in any way except to say that he was watching over her little girl, Lana tried to make herself think of nothing except enjoying the salty breeze and Maggie's laughter as her little girl played with Trent.

Sometimes you just had to pull a Scarlett O'Hara and save your worrying for tomorrow, so you didn't waste the day you'd been given. That was a lesson that cancer had taught her very early in life.

Trent hung up the phone after listening to his father's message right before he turned into Lana's drive. He had known his father would be curious about his missing the latest board meeting of Montgomery and Lord, and that it was just a matter of time before his father started to make inquiries into his absence.

He had to make a decision about whether to continue with his plans or to trust Lana with the information that as of now was only known by him and his lawyer.

It had seemed so simple when he had first decided to come to Florida and get custody of his niece. First he would hire a nanny and make sure the child was taken care of. Then he'd approach his father with his brother's will and make sure the old man knew that he no longer had any power to manipulate others the way he had his wife and younger son.

Trent got out of the car and smoothed his dark dress pants as he tried to clear his mind of all the pain and anger that immediately consumed him when he thought of his father. The old man had a lot to answer for, and for the first time in his life Trent might have the means of making him pay for his sins.

But first he had to decide what to do about Lana. Could he trust her to understand the danger his father was to Maggie? More importantly, would she trust *him* if she learned about the stipulations in Michael's will?

He had no explanation for the intimate tug he felt drawing them closer together, but it was easy to see that the physical attraction between them made Lana uncomfortable. With the little he had learned about her he knew she was as much out of her comfort zone with him as he was with her.

He had felt her pull away from him as soon as they had left the beach and he hadn't liked it. After Maggie had fallen asleep in her car seat Lana had been quiet until they had arrived back at her place, where she had very curtly thanked him for the trip to the beach. Then she had stated that she didn't think it was a good idea for them to go out to dinner together.

He'd somehow managed to turn the conversation around, though, so that she had agreed to go out with him tonight to "discuss their options" in relation to Maggie. He couldn't help but smile when he thought of that clipped tone her voice took on when she turned all Momma Bear on him.

He ran his hands through his hair and let out

a heartfelt groan. Why was he rethinking all his carefully laid plans *now*? It had been a lot easier to think of taking his niece away from some stranger than it was to execute that plan now. The more time he spent with Lana the harder it was going to be to take Maggie away from her.

It seemed as if his plan to stick close to Lana and Maggie was starting to backfire on him and he only had himself to blame.

Maggie checked the mirror one last time, turning to get a view of the way the black dress followed the curve of her hips, stopping a few inches before reaching the back of her knees. Turning back around, she admired the way the jeweled neckline that circled her neck sparkled. It had been a long time since she had dressed up for a date. Okay, so maybe it wasn't really a date, but she still deserved a little mirror-time.

"You look hot," Amanda said from where she sat on the edge of the bed. "Doesn't Mommy look hot, Maggie?"

"Hot?" Maggie asked, giving Lana a questioning look.

"No, Mommy's not hot," Lana said as she picked up the sweet-smelling toddler and snuggled her close. Nothing could be as angelic as a freshly bathed toddler all ready for bed.

"See?" Lana told Maggie as she tickled her belly. "Not hot."

"I'll have to ask Trent his opinion when he arrives," Amanda said, reaching over to take the toddler.

"You do and I'll tell that resident on the oncology floor that you were ogling his backside the other day when I stopped by."

"I was not… Okay, maybe I was." Amanda giggled. "But have you seen how cute he is in those scrubs?"

"Yeah," Lana said "it was all the nurses could talk about until…"

"Until the cowboy doctor showed up?" Amanda teased. "Too bad for them that the only person he seems to be looking back at is you."

"He just wants to get to know his niece," Lana said. "That's all it is," she insisted as she saw Amanda's expression in the mirror. "The only reason I agreed to go tonight was to see if

I could find out more about him," she said. "I need all the ammunition I can get in this fight."

"Are you trying to convince me or yourself?" Amanda said as she hurried off to answer the door.

"Behave!" Lana called after her friend.

The last thing she needed was for Amanda to insinuate that there was something romantic going on between them. There was too much tension between them as it was. She didn't need Trent thinking that she was like all the other nurses in the hospital, who had joined the Team Trent fan club.

She would go out tonight and listen to what he had to say, and then she would get her turn to explain to the man why her daughter needed to stay with *her.*

CHAPTER FIVE

TRENT HAD KNOWN he was in trouble the minute Lana had stepped into the tiny living room wearing that sexy as hell black dress. His hands had clenched with the need to explore the body wrapped up in all that slinky black material and the woman dressed in the package hadn't had a clue what she was doing to him.

She had stood there in her living room, with that same sweet smile of hers that screamed innocence, while every delicious curve of her had sent him into sexual overdrive. Then there were those ridiculously high gold heels that had her almost coming up to stand eye to eye to him. Did she have *any* idea what having her lips that much closer to his was doing to him?

If it had been one of his usual dating partners he'd have had no doubt that this was a calculated move to reel him in—but this woman? No, one of the things he found so surprising about her was her honesty. She said what she thought and expected the same of others. She didn't play crazy games that ended up causing hurt feelings and resentment.

As a young man he'd learned quickly that there were women in the world who would use their bodies to manipulate you if you gave them a chance. It was something he did not put up with. He'd seen enough drama in his life as a child with his parents; he didn't need any in his adult life.

It was going to be a long night, he decided as he joined Lana in the car and headed for the restaurant.

As they drove he kept the conversation to common small talk as he tried to get his body under control—something he found almost impossible with her sitting close beside him. Keeping his eyes on the road, he reminded his overheated body of all the complications getting involved with her would cause.

He was relieved to find that by the time they drove up to the entrance and he handed his keys over to the valet the self-control he depended on had taken over once more. He couldn't afford to show any sign of weakness to Lana.

* * *

Lana took her seat at the linen-draped table. Except for discussing his choice of the newest Brazilian steak house in town, they'd kept their conversation to discussions of work and weather. She waited until the waiter had taken their orders and moved away before trying to turn the conversation to a more personal topic.

"So, are you missing Houston yet?" she asked.

Maybe if she could get him talking about his home he'd open up more about his brother. She had to figure out if there was more to his seeking out Maggie and moving to Miami. She could understand he would have an interest in seeing that his niece was being taken care of, but most unmarried men would have made a fast check on the child then flown out of town as soon as possible.

But not Trent. No, he had dug in with both feet in this custody battle. Somehow she just knew there was more going on than she was aware of. Just the mention of his brother and he turned to stone. Was he grieving? Yes, she was sure there was pain in his eyes when the subject came up, but there was much more that he was keeping to himself. It was the key to his being here in Miami and she wanted to know just what he was holding back from her.

"I miss my colleagues, and of course I miss Tanglefoot," Trent answered.

"Tanglefoot?" Lana asked. "Is that the name of some sort of animal or do you have a very clumsy friend?"

"She's a very stubborn horse," Trent said, "but I love her."

Lana watched the smile that lit his face as some unshared memory seemed to come to his mind. It was nice to see the man truly relax and lower those shields he kept up between himself and others. Or was it just *her* that he was trying to keep out?

They each chose a selection of meat from the platter one of the gauchos was serving from and then continued.

"So, where does Tanglefoot stay?" Lana asked. Maybe if she kept him on what seemed like a safe subject he would finally open up to her.

"She's at my family's ranch," Trent said.

"But you live in the city, right?" Lana asked between bites of thinly sliced beef.

"I have a place in the city, but I try to get away at least once a week," Trent answered. "I spend as much of my off-time helping around the ranch as possible"

"Like what? Riding fences and looking for stray cattle?" Lana asked.

"Yeah, some…" Trent answered.

"Really?" Lana asked.

Trent gave one of his killer smiles that had her imagining him in his jeans and boots. She had no problem envisioning him on his horse, waving his hat as he rode off into the sunset.

"There's only a few hundred head of cattle left now. My father is more interested in the oil industry. But the ranch has been in my mother's family for a long time, so I try to keep an eye on the place. I like to spend time with the horses and do some of the necessary maintenance around the place."

"I can't really see you as a handyman," Lana said. No, she definitely saw him more as a cowboy.

"I might surprise you," Trent said, and flashed her another one of his potent smiles. "I'm pretty good with my hands."

Lana looked down at her plate, trying to ignore his intended innuendo. She wasn't stupid, and she had noticed that any time she started making headway into his personal life he turned on that flirty charm of his. It might work with some women, but she wasn't about to fall for it.

Not that she was unaffected by the thought of his hands. She had no doubt that those hands were very talented, and she'd seen how gentle they could be when he held tiny newborn babies…

"What?" she asked when she allowed herself to look up from her plate and caught his amused look.

"I like that flustered look you get whenever you're embarrassed," Trent said. "And then there's the blush…"

She had felt warmth spread through her cheeks barely a second before his comment. How did he *do* that? It was if he had been studying her and knew her responses even before she did. Was she that transparent?

"Sorry," Trent said. "I really didn't mean to embarrass you."

"I was asking you about the ranch," Lana said.

"Yes, you were."

"You mentioned your dad…what about your mom?"

Lana noted the change in Trent immediately. All joking was gone now and sadness touched his eyes.

"She passed away when me and Michael were still kids," Trent answered.

"I'm sorry," Lana said.

Reaching over, she covered his hand with hers. Though it had been a long time since his mother's death, she could tell he was still grieving. Some deaths were like that. They touched you forever. She had seen it in patients who had lost a child many years earlier.

For a second the thought of losing Maggie crossed her mind. She closed the door on those thoughts quickly. She wouldn't go there tonight.

"Thanks, but it was a long time ago."

"It had to have been hard on the two of you," she said.

"Especially Michael—he was so young that I don't think he even had many memories of her," Trent said.

"But you do. I'd think it would have been harder on you, really knowing what was missing from your life," she said as she removed her hand and went back to her meal. Even with his mother's death, Trent was determined to put his brother before himself.

"Maybe, but then again I have memories. He didn't."

"So who took care of you when the two of you were growing up?"

"My great-aunt Flo came to live with us. My mother's aunt. She still lives there."

Trent watched as Lana pushed back her plate so that the restaurant staff would stop the continuous flow of food to their table. He ordered a coffee for himself when she turned down dessert, then leaned back in his chair. The tension that had been with him when they had started the evening had drained to only a tinge of discomfort now centered in his upper shoulders.

He rolled his head to ease the pulling on his muscles. He had been worried when Lana had started with the questions about his brother, but though he usually didn't discuss much of his personal life with others, talking with Lana hadn't been the uncomfortable conversation he might have thought it would be. Not that he hadn't recognized all this interest in his life for what it was: Lana was fishing for anything she could use against him.

"You look tired," Lana commented. "Are we working you too hard?"

Was that concern in her voice? How could she possibly care about how he was doing when he had brought all kinds of trouble into her life?

"I'm fine," Trent said.

He was about to leave it at that when he saw a flicker of distress flash through her eyes. Taking a slow, deep breath, to prepare himself to be hit with all her accusations, he continued.

"I'm sorry, Lana. I know my coming into your life like this has to be a nightmare," Trent said. "I bet you wish I'd get on the first plane out of town."

"I was thinking more like you would ride off into the sunset, Cowboy."

He watched as a small twitch played at the corner of her mouth, then she looked down at her hands, which were tangled in the napkin in her lap.

"I can't say what I would do if I found out my brother had a kid out there I hadn't been told about, but that doesn't make the position you've put me in any easier. Haven't you wondered why Chloe picked me to give Maggie to?" Lana asked. "She could have gone with any one of a dozen private adoption lawyers in town, but she came to *me*."

"I know you were her midwife," Trent answered.

"I was." Lana said. "And you must know how sometimes you just develop a bond with your patient? When they just seem to touch something inside of you? That part of you that you feel you have to protect, because you know if you let it the heartbreak you see every day will cause you to burn out, and then you wouldn't be able to help anyone anymore?"

Trent nodded his head toward her. He'd learned at an early age that you had to keep those feelings that left you vulnerable to the outside world locked up inside, where they couldn't be used against you, and during his clinical rotations he had been able to put up the walls that protected him. Until he had started his pediatric rotation. It had been the young ones, the innocent ones so filled with hope and trust, that he hadn't been able to help but feel his heart soften toward.

And wasn't that what was happening with

the woman sitting across from him? Somehow, no matter how he built up those walls he knew he needed to keep erected between them, she could find a way over, around or through them. And that made her a weakness he couldn't afford.

"I knew Chloe was all alone in town—she told me when I first saw her in the office. And she had been very open about her addiction problem with prescription drugs, and about her rehab and methadone treatment. But it really wasn't until after Maggie was born that I got to know her."

"Ms. Nelson at Children and Families told me about Maggie's withdrawal," Trent said.

"You know how that is. It's like going through hell when someone goes through withdrawal. Watching an adult patient go through it is hard enough, but watching a baby… Maggie…" Lana stopped and reached for her glass.

The tremble in her hand as she raised her glass to her mouth told him that Maggie had to have been really sick. He'd seen infants go through withdrawal many times, and it was a horror for the staff as well as the parents. He could only imagine how hard it had been for Lana to watch Maggie experiencing the pain and agitation her withdrawal would have caused. The thought of it had him clenching his fists.

Why were children always the ones who had to pay for the mistakes of their parents? It was a question that had haunted him for years as he had watched his brother's drinking spiral out of control.

"I'd find Chloe sitting beside Maggie's crib in the neonatal unit, just staring at her baby. She looked so lost and alone that I found myself sitting with her there, talking to her for longer and longer each day."

Lana looked up at Trent, capturing his eyes with hers until he felt himself drawn into her sorrow.

"I'm not trying to make excuses for her. But after Maggie got out of withdrawal, when Chloe decided she couldn't take the stress of caring for her, she did the most unselfish thing she could do. She put the care and wellbeing of her baby first. I can't imagine what it took for her to come to my house the night she brought Maggie to me," Lana continued. "And I'll admit I'm not nearly as brave. I can't give Maggie up.

I *won't* give her up," Lana said as she rose from her chair.

Trent could see the pleading in her eyes, the innocent hope that shone out of them, asking for his help. She could have asked him for anything right then. Anything except for what she needed—his assurance that everything would be all right. Of course it wouldn't. They both knew that. Only one of them could win custody of Maggie, and right now he wasn't sure who he was hoping that would be.

It was only knowing the harm that his father could do to both Maggie *and* Lana that assured him he was doing the right thing.

"I saw them myself!"

"Saw who?" Lana asked as she walked into the nurses' break room.

She watched as two of the nurses who had been in there excused themselves. The other four nurses were either looking down at the floor or at Kat, the department's queen of gossip.

"We were just talking about what we did on our time off," said Laurie, the charge nurse.

"Did *you* do anything exciting this weekend?" Kat asked, and leaned toward Lana.

The room suddenly became quiet and everyone in turned toward her expectantly. It was becoming very obvious that there was some piece of information they were all waiting for her to share. And by the way they all seemed to be anticipating her answer she knew this wasn't a casual question.

And then it hit her. Someone had seen her out with Trent. And that someone was apparently Kat, who she could see had been only too happy to run back and share the news with her colleagues.

She couldn't blame them for their interest. While the hospital was quite large, they were still a tight-knit group who seemed to share everything with each other—even things that were really none of their business. But that didn't mean she was prepared to go into details about her and Trent's relationship.

She had enough problems keeping Trent and her court case from interfering with their work relationship. So far her explanation that a last-minute complication had temporarily postponed Maggie's adoption had been all the reason she had needed. No one knew that the "complication" was Trent—or at least if they did she hadn't heard any talk about it. If it got out there that they were seeing each other socially, the gossip fire would be raging out of control. There was no way she was going to give it any more fuel.

"Nothing special. I just took Maggie to the beach Saturday. She loved it, of course. Besides that it was just a normal weekend."

Lana almost laughed at the look of disappointment on the group's faces. There would be more talk when she left the room, she was sure. And if Kat ws being her imaginative self by the end of the day she was also sure the hospital would be full of gossip about her and Trent's torrid affair. She'd have to warn him, but besides that she decided just to ignore it.

"Laurie—Hannah Bowers has texted me that she is on her way," Lana told the charge nurse. "Hopefully she's just having Braxton Hicks contractions."

"How many weeks is she now?" Laurie asked as she got up and began to clear the space where she had been eating.

"She was thirty-six last Friday, when I saw

her," Lana answered. "I checked her cervix and she was thinning out, but not dilated yet."

"Thirty-six is pretty good for twins," Kat commented.

"We won't stop her if she's in labor," Lana said. "Just call me when she comes in and I'll come over and do an exam."

Hoping that the excitement of possibly having a twin delivery would give the staff something to talk about besides her love-life, Lana headed back to her office to catch up on her daily appointments.

The prospect of a twin delivery thrilled her too, but she'd have to use some good time management or things would back up fast in the office.

Lana had only managed to see a couple of patients before Laurie called to say that Hannah had arrived with her mother and was having contractions.

After signing out with the office she made the quick walk over to the labor unit. Looking at the contraction pattern of two minutes apart, Lana wasn't surprised to find Hannah's cervical exam showing that she was definitely in labor.

"Ready to meet these two?" Lana asked as she motioned toward Hannah's stretched belly.

"Really?" Hannah asked. "I've got to call Jimmy. Momma—you call him. I've had so many false alarms that he'll never believe me."

"Probably would be a good idea to go ahead and make that call," Lana said. "You're progressing pretty well. When did the contractions start?"

"Just before Jimmy left for work. I didn't want to tell him. He'd have insisted on staying home and I didn't want him to miss work. Are they okay?" Hannah asked as she indicated the monitor screen, where four different lines graphed out, each in a different color.

"Their heart-rates look great," Lana answered. "They're early, but it's not unusual for twins to come early."

"Probably because they've run out of room in there," Hannah said as she rubbed her large belly.

"I'm going to order an ultrasound. I can tell that Baby Anna is presenting with her head down, but I need to check on James Junior,"

Lana said. "I know we discussed you trying for a vaginal delivery…"

"If I can," Hannah said.

"Is that safe?" asked Hannah's mother. "When my sister had her twins they just cut her and took them out."

The middle-aged woman came to stand near her daughter and Lana could see the concern in the woman's eyes.

"Things have changed since then, Momma," Hannah said as she reached over and took her mother's hand. "Remember one of the girls at your church delivered her twins vaginally?"

"I'll wait for the ultrasound results and then I'll talk with the obstetrician on call. If both twins are positioned correctly it will be okay to let the labor continue to progress," Lana said. "But don't forget—if the second baby decides to change position after we deliver the first, you probably will end up with a Cesarean section."

"You mean she could have *both*?" Hannah's mother asked as she got up from her chair and walked over to the monitors to study the readings.

"Momma worries," Hannah explained.

"And I don't blame her one bit," Lana said

as she headed for the door. "I'm going to go get that ultrasound ordered now. You just get Jimmy on his way here, and after the ultrasound we'll all get together to decide how we're going to go from here. I also think you should consider going ahead and getting an epidural."

"This soon?" Hannah asked as she shifted in the bed.

Lana watched as the contraction that was tracing on the monitor peaked, then slowly went down. She had noticed Hannah instinctively take deeper breaths as the contractions had come and gone.

"You're going to need one soon. We can get some IV fluids going too, so that you'll be ready when Anesthesia gets here."

"Thanks, Lana," Hannah said.

"And just remember," Lana said when she reached the door. "The most important thing today isn't *how* you deliver—it's that we end up with two healthy babies and a healthy momma."

As she shut the door she heard Hannah's nervous mother say, "Amen." She couldn't blame her for having concerns about her daughter. Even knowing everything she knew about childbirth, Lana still knew that if it were her Maggie in there she would be a nervous wreck.

But what if she wasn't around when Maggie grew up and had children of her own?

That thought had her stopping to lean against the nearest wall. She took a deep breath that would have made any labor doula proud, and let it out slowly as she tried to calm herself. She was starting to have more and more periods of anxiety over the custody case, and was afraid that one day she was going to find herself in a full-blown panic attack.

And how would *that* look to the court? And to Trent? He was always so in control of his emotions. He would never understand what she was going through. There had to be something she could do to help ease the anxiety she was feeling.

Of course the only thing that would really help would be Trent dropping his petition with the court and returning to Texas, so that she and Maggie could get back to their life together.

Yes, Trent leaving would be the answer to all her troubles—but what could she do to make that happen? She'd shown him that Maggie was happy and safe with her. He had to be able to see how much she loved her little girl. What more did he want?

And to top everything off she *didn't* need the complication of her hormones going crazy every time she was around the man. There had never been a man she was so sexually aware of in her life, and it made her feel self-conscious and unsure of herself at a time when she needed to be portraying someone who was totally confident in her life.

She took another deep breath to help cleanse her thoughts, then continued down the hall. She'd call her mother tonight. Between sharing her heartache with her momma and a pint of chocolate ice cream she would surely come up with some strategy to get her through the next couple of weeks.

Trent entered the labor and delivery unit and went in search of Lana. He was telling himself he needed to get an update on her patient's condition so he'd know how soon he and the nursery team would be needed, but he knew it was just an excuse to go and see the midwife. He hadn't seen her since their night out, and he had already planned to hunt her down later that day to make more arrangements to see Maggie.

Of course he could have just called to set that up, but that wasn't what he wanted.

What was it about her that had caught his interest and refused to let it go? She was certainly a beautiful woman, with her seductive curves and that thick blond mane of hers, and those green eyes that filled with love when she talked about Maggie. But he had dated plenty of beautiful women who hadn't affected him like she did. Even Maria hadn't captivated him the way Lana did, and Maria had been the perfect woman.

Maria had been everything he had wanted in a woman—beautiful, smart, and most importantly independent. He'd never had to worry about her throwing a fit if he got called into work, or complaining about him not spending enough time with her. If he'd been late for a social function due to a case going long she'd never been angry with him.

It had been the perfect relationship and he had been surprised when, after dating him for several months, she had called him one day to tell him she wouldn't be seeing him anymore—

that she wanted to see other people and didn't feel that he could give her what she needed out of a relationship.

While he couldn't say that she had broken his heart, he *had* been hurt. No, he'd never felt that all-consuming love everyone talked about, but he had cared about her.

He'd seen her a few weeks later in a corner of the hospital cafeteria, holding the hand of one of the residents. Stopping to study them for a moment, he'd noted the flush of Maria's face and the way those deep brown eyes of hers had never left the young man. He had waited for jealousy to fill him, but he'd felt nothing.

It was then he'd realized that, no matter how intimate they had been, what they'd had was just a close friendship and nothing more. Maria had realized that too and wanted more. He hadn't.

And that brought him back to Lana. The two of them had managed to create a good working relationship and, even with everything between them, if not a friendship at least they'd managed a truce. He didn't want to endanger that because of some misplaced attraction between the two of them. Maybe if she was another woman they'd be able to scratch the itch and move on, but everything he'd learned about Lana told him that wasn't her way.

Lana was the kind of woman who would want roses and candles before she became in any way involved with someone, and then she'd be wanting the house with the white picket fence. She had quickly shown him that she was all about family, which put her at the top of his list of women to stay away from.

He'd learned a long time ago that he didn't have anything to give a woman other than his friendship and sex, and that was enough for him. He had no desire to be responsible for someone else's happiness. He'd heard his mother's claims of love for his father and it had destroyed not only her but the rest of their family. He never wanted to get caught in that trap, where everything depended on someone's feeling for you or your feelings for them.

He owed Lana a lot for taking care of his niece, and he wouldn't repay her by letting her think there could be more between them than there was. He was already trying to take the baby she loved away from her, and he knew that already made him just as much of a cold bastard as his father.

He'd found himself wrestling with that fact each night when he lay in his bed. On one hand he wanted to leave Maggie with Lana, knowing that she would always be loved and taken care of. But on the other hand Michael had asked him in his will to take care of the little girl. Couldn't Lana understand that he had to honor his brother's request?

And then there was Maggie's inheritance… So far Michael's lawyer had been able to stall his father concerning the contents of his brother's will, but he knew his father would have his own lawyers looking into it soon.

No one except for him and his brother's lawyers knew that upon gaining custody of Maggie he, Trent, would have control of the majority of the shares to Montgomery and Lord, but if his father found out that little tidbit before the custody case was settled he knew Maggie would be in danger of being used like everyone else Calvin Montgomery touched, and he couldn't let that happen to another person he cared about.

It was up to him to protect his niece and he

was going to have to find a way to make Lana understand—even if it meant airing some of his family's dirty laundry. And there was plenty of that.

Trent was about to give up on finding Lana when he saw her in the nurses' break room. For a moment he just watched as she laughed with the two labor nurses she was sharing her lunch with. It was nice to see her laughing with her friends. With all the stress he had added to her life, it was amazing that she could still relax for a moment. And no matter how much he told himself the woman was dangerous, he had to admit he enjoyed looking at her.

"Excuse me," Trent said as he interrupted the three of them in their meal. "I was wondering if I could see you for just a minute, Lana?"

He stepped out through the door to let her pass, and was surprised when she grabbed his arm and pulled him down the hall to one of the empty exam rooms.

"What are you *doing*?" she asked him in a voice not much over a whisper.

"I'm not sure," he whispered back as he looked down to where Lana was still gripping his arm. "And why are we whispering?"

Lana dropped his arm. “Do you know who that was I was eating with?”

“Well, I know Kat…” Trent said.

“Of *course* you do,” Lana said, then walked across the room away from him.

“What does that mean?” he said as he followed her.

“Nothing,” she said.

Trent watched her as she stood there with her arms crossed, glaring at him while she chewed at her bottom lip. Then, as if coming to some conclusion—although on what he had no clue—she marched up to him.

“Kat is the biggest gossiper in the unit—probably in the whole hospital, for that matter,” Lana said.

“And I should be concerned about that… why?” Trent asked.

Was the man dense? Lana had been tiptoeing around questions about her weekend all day, and then he’d walked right into the break room and asked to speak to her. By now everybody on the floor would be speculating about what was going on between the two of them.

“Because somebody saw us out together the

other night, and now everyone has got it into their head that there's something going on between us."

Lana watched as that information hit him. And then the stupid man smiled.

"It's not funny!" she said as she punched him in the arm.

"Ouch," he said, rubbing his arm.

"Will you just be serious for a moment?" Lana asked. "The last thing I want is for everyone to find out that there's something going on between us."

Lana watched as Trent sobered. He leaned back and then sat on the tightly made hospital bed.

"And what exactly *is* going on between us?" Trent asked.

"They don't know about your brother, or the reason my adoption of Maggie has been put on hold," she said. "I don't want to have to walk around this hospital with everybody talking about it."

She'd had enough of those pity-filled stares when she was a bald-headed teenager after her chemo and radiation treatments. She didn't want to live through that again.

"Sorry," he said. "I just wanted to ask you about this weekend—about me seeing Maggie."

Lana stopped and looked at him. He hadn't meant to cause trouble. It wasn't his fault that tongues were wagging.

"No, *I'm* sorry," she said. "I shouldn't be so sensitive."

Walking across the room she took a seat beside him, and for a few seconds they sat there together in silence. She was starting to realize that in some ways Trent was just as much a victim in this nightmare of a court case as she was. *He* hadn't left Maggie's mother when she was pregnant. He hadn't come to Miami to stop her adopting Maggie for himself. Everything he was doing was for his brother.

While it was easy for her to see that taking Maggie away from the only home she had ever known was not the right thing for the child, she knew he was just trying to do what he thought was best for his niece—even though she knew he was wrong.

"Let me check my call schedule for the weekend…"

"Oh, *there* you two are," Kat said as she stuck her head in the door. "Dr. Miller called for an update on Hannah's progress. I told him I couldn't find you, but that I'd be glad to have you call him back."

Lana looked at Trent before jumping down off the bed. By the silly smile he gave her as she left the room she knew he was aware of just what the next set of rumors would be. She'd have some explaining to do to the people she worked with if they got wind of the fact that the two of them had been caught together on one of the hospital beds.

Because one look at Trent and no one would believe they were innocent. At least no female would.

CHAPTER SIX

WITH HANNAH'S TWINS in the right position, they decided to go through with a vaginal delivery. As soon as Hannah was fully dilated and ready to push, they moved her to an operating room to deliver in case there were any complications.

Lana saw Trent dressed in his scrubs helping the nursery team set up when she entered after scrubbing up.

"Twins, huh?" Trent said.

"You don't do vaginal delivery of twins in Texas?" she asked.

"We do. Just most of ours are delivered by doctors," he said.

"I've done several, and Dr. Miller is on standby in the unit in case the second baby decides to misbehave. Trust me—I've got this," she said with a smile, then winked at him.

She knew the adrenaline rush was making her cocky and hoped she didn't regret the words later.

* * *

Trent watched as Lana moved over to her patient and couldn't help but smile back. If the look on her face was any indication, Lana had certainly found her calling in midwifery. While she was definitely full of confidence, he saw that she checked through the instruments arranged for the double vaginal delivery, as well as checking that she had everything they'd need if things changed and they had to do a C-section.

After having one of the nurses confirm that Dr. Miller, the obstetrician, was on the unit and available, she had Hannah start to push.

Several minutes later the first twin started to crown and Trent gowned and prepared for the delivery. when Lana handed the crying little girl to him, he carried her over to the warmer and checked her out from head to toe. She was a bit small for her gestation, but nothing that wouldn't be expected in a twin.

One of the nurses name-banded and bundled the baby, then carried it over to the waiting father.

Lana was busy doing an ultrasound on her

patient. “Okay, Hannah and Jimmy—you ready to meet James Junior?”

Hannah nodded her head excitedly, then started to push again. Trent had to give it to the woman—and to women in general. He didn’t know a man alive who would be able to go through what these mothers did.

With the top of a second little head crowning after a few pushes, he watched as Lana carefully delivered the head, then the shoulders.

“James Junior’s been stealing the food from his sister,” she said as she held the much larger baby boy up for them to see.

She cut the cord, then handed the newest member of the family to Trent. Within seconds of stimulating him with a firm rub on his back he had the baby boy as pink and as loud as his sister.

“Congratulations!” Trent said later, as Lana took a seat on one of the benches across from him in the locker room.

“Thanks. How are the babies?” Lana asked.

“They’re doing good. They’re both with their parents. We’re watching their sugars, but besides the extreme difference in size they’re perfect," he said. "The nurses are all talking about how good you did. And I didn't hear a word about us being caught in bed together."

Lana made a face at him and then broke down in giggles. She knew she was still on an adrenaline high from the delivery, but it felt good to just relax and enjoy it for a minute. Today was a day to celebrate the two new lives that had come into the world. Nothing could be better for renewing a person's hope in life than seeing a baby starting out it's life.

Trent watched her as she talked about what a privilege it was to be a part of the twins delivery. Joy seemed to flow out of her as she described the two babies who had just come into the world.

It was as if the beauty that he had learned was inside her was blooming out into her sparkling green eyes. Her cheeks glowed bright with color from her excitement and he had never been so turned on by just watching a woman talk.

He felt something in him thaw as the beautiful sound of her laughter touched him in a place he had closed up inside himself years ago. Her laughter warmed him and her smile teased him into wanting more. Would it be so bad just to enjoy this moment without worrying about all the complications that could follow?

Realizing she was on the point of blabbering, Lana stopped and looked up to see Trent had come to stand in front of her. Gone was the man who had earlier in the day joked with her about her concerns over gossiping nurses. The playful teasing she had become accustomed to had been replaced by a dangerous intensity that seemed to fill him, leaving his body taut with tension and reminding her of a wild cat preparing to pounce.

Everything about him had become hard now—everything except for his eyes.

Lana stood and moved closer, as if drawn into them. They seemed a deeper blue today. A blue she knew she would drown in if she wasn't careful. Then Trent took a step forward and his eyes went from calm sea to hungry storm—a storm that had the power either to pull her in or toss her away.

Fear about which he would choose, and what she herself wanted, had her taking a step back and moving around the wooden bench that penned her into the tight space.

"Trent?" she heard herself say, the sound barely audible as if it came from far away.

When he ignored her plea and took a second and then another step toward her, instinct had her continuing her retreat until she felt the door against her back.

She held herself still as he reached around her and locked the door. The warmth of his breath fanned her face, and when she glanced up at his lips she was surprised to find them so close to hers. So close that she could feel the warmth of them.

No longer willing to wait for his advance, she pushed up on her toes and met his mouth with hers. A white heat scorched her as it rushed through her body, then puddled in her core. The excitement of the twin delivery was scattered away as a new, more dangerous thrill filled her. Soon hard lips were meeting soft tongues as they battled, both of them advancing and retreating.

She felt Trent's hands as they skimmed over her back, then came to rest on her hips. He pulled her body closer until she felt the length of his erection as it rested between her legs. When he pushed himself against her, pinning her against the door, she was left with no doubt as to what he wanted. What they both wanted.

As their mouths continued to war she felt herself surrender to him. He was hard for her and she was aching to let him take her. Right then. Right there. Against the locker room door.

The memory of where they were suddenly broke through her clouded mind. She was about to have sex in a locker room. In the middle of the day. With the man who was trying to take her daughter away from her.

For a second Trent ignored her when she tried to pull away.

"Trent," she said when she managed to free her mouth, "we've got to stop."

She felt his fingers relax on her hips, but still he didn't move.

"I guess we were about to give the staff something to *really* talk about," Trent said as he rested his chin on the top of her head, so that her face was cradled against his chest.

Lana took a deep breath in, enjoying the tangy scent of hot and bothered male. She would take that smell with her. But it was *all* she could take of him. She had never been a woman who could handle a sex-only relationship. She needed more from a man. But with her body still aching for his she knew she had to get away from him.

"I've got to go," Lana said as she shifted against him.

"You never answered my question," Trent said.

She pulled back and looked up at him.

"What *is* going on between the two of us?" he asked.

"Nothing," she answered, then looked away, afraid that her eyes would show a longing for something more that she knew she couldn't have.

"If that was nothing, I don't know if I could live through your something," he said, with a touch of humor that surprised her.

He held her to him for just a second longer before he released her and moved away.

"I got a call earlier from Ms. Nelson," he said.

With the mention of the social worker's name the warmth that had been between them faded. *This* was why she knew the right thing to do was to step back from Trent. Anything that they could possibly have would never survive the battle they would soon find themselves in.

"What did she say?" Lana said as she tried to stomp down on the panic that wanted to rise up and take control.

"Nothing that we weren't expecting. The DNA testing came back. I'm Maggie's uncle, Lana," Trent said. "Maggie's a Montgomery."

She watched him reach down and lift his duffle bag onto his shoulder. She walked across the room and kicked off her shoes. Feeling a bit shaky, she sat on the bench in front of her locker. She took her time changing into her street shoes and storing her work pair, and by the time she looked up the door was shutting, leaving her alone with even more questions than she'd had before.

Lana walked into the social worker's office knowing she was a coward. She had spent the week avoiding Trent as much as possible. The few times they had ended up on the labor unit at the same time she had made a fast retreat to her office.

If only it was that easy to run away from the dreams that haunted her nights, leaving her in tangled sheets with an unsatisfied need that filled her days.

She could deny that there was anything between them to Trent, but she wasn't able to lie to herself. She was letting herself get too close to him and that was dangerous. She couldn't allow herself to put anything before her family right now. She had to be totally professional from now on, and that meant no nights out with Trent and no moments alone together.

Then he walked into the room, and all her determination to keep things strictly business between them fled. How was she supposed to ignore this man who could turn her libido into a hormonal teenager's just by entering the room?

Dressed in soft gray dress pants and a black polo shirt, he had the look of a wealthy oil tycoon, with his charcoal cowboy boots and the black Stetson hat he held in his hands. She remembered the night at the restaurant, when he had told her about working on the family ranch and joked about how good he was with his hands.

The room suddenly heated up with her memories of those hands holding her in place while he pressed himself tight against her, his lips hot against hers. His hands were not the only things he was good with…

"Ms. Nelson… Lana," he said as he took the seat next to her.

"Thanks for coming down," the social worker said. "I think the two of you have gotten the information on the DNA testing from your lawyers?"

She continued when they each nodded their heads.

"I just wanted to get the two of you together to discuss how the visitations are going and to let you know what our plans are from here forward. I've talked with Nathan, Lana, and he has told me you're planning on continuing with the adoption."

"Yes, I plan on continuing with my plans for custody of Maggie," Lana said, hoping she had managed to keep the tremble she felt out of her voice.

"And I will need to continue with my petition also," Trent said.

"And your visitations with Maggie?" asked Ms. Nelson.

"We've done very well together," Trent commented, then looked over at Lana. "At least I think so."

"Trent is very good with Maggie," Lana answered. "He had no problem winning Maggie over. I think he's a natural in the uncle department."

"Well, thank you, ma'am," Trent said in his deepest Texan drawl.

Lana tried to stop the smile that always came when he was in this cute flirty mood.

"I think he just can't help charming every female he meets," she said.

"What?" Trent said. "I want you to know I take my wooing of a woman very seriously."

"*Wooing?* Who uses a word like 'wooing?'" she said as she turned back to Trent. "What does that even mean?"

"Well, I can tell you that any woman I woo will definitely know what it means."

Ms. Nelson cleared her throat and they both turned toward the social worker, who was looking at them as if they had lost their minds.

"The visitations are going well," Lana said, and she sat back in her seat, then looked down at her hands.

"So I see," the social worker said, and gave them a friendly smile.

Lana took a deep breath and decided to dive into the speech she had prepared on her way to the office. She made sure that when she looked up she avoided looking at Trent. She locked her eyes on the older woman and hoped to see some understanding in the gray eyes that met hers.

"Trent can come to visit Maggie as often as he wants—" Lana started.

"Thanks," Trent said.

"Let me finish," Lana said. "But while I plan on continuing Trent's visits with Maggie…"

From her seat beside him Lana felt the tension as it coiled through him and he visibly straightened in his chair. This wasn't going to be easy, but she had to have her say. Squaring her shoulders, she moved up to the edge of her seat and began again. She had practiced, she had memorized, and she *would* get through this.

"Trent will always be Maggie's uncle, and I will always allow him to see his niece," said Lana. She let the breath she had been holding out and took in another one, this one deeper, as she tried to get her thoughts together. "But with all the things Trent can provide for her, the one thing he can't provide is something every little girl needs. A mother."

"Are you saying a single father can't raise a child?" Trent asked. "Aren't fathers important too?"

"No. I mean, yes." Lana fumbled over the words as she tried to ignore the anger she could hear rising in Trent's voice. "Yes. Fathers are important. But Maggie's being raised with a mother figure. I'm all she's ever known. What happens when you take that away from her? What happens when she wakes up in the middle of the night crying and I'm not there, Trent?"

"It sounds to me like what she really needs is the both of you," Ms. Nelson interrupted, and then continued before either of them could comment. "Trent, I need to discuss a few matters with you, if you have a few more minutes? I appreciate you coming down to see me, Lana, and I understand your concerns. If you need anything, or have any questions, you know you can give me a call."

Lana stood and thanked the social worker before leaving the office. She had been dismissed.

Turning back, she saw the woman get up and shut her office door. She couldn't help feeling as if she was being shut out of something that might have a big impact on her little girl. She turned and headed for the elevators, trying to decide how she would get through the next few days while she waited to see what step the courts would take next.

"I think you can understand Lana's concerns," Ms. Nelson said.

Trent took a long look at the social worker. She wore a friendly concerned look that he knew must put her clients at ease, but she was shrewd too. She knew how to get information when she needed it to get her job done.

"I do understand where Lana is coming from," Trent said.

"What we need to remember here is that a little girl's future is about to be determined and it is our responsibility to make the best decision we can in her interests. Anything besides honesty between the three of us would be going against what is best for Maggie."

Trent nodded his head in agreement, then waited for the social worker to continue. He had agreed to be honest with her. He tried to push back the guilt he felt about keeping information about his brother's will from both the social worker and from Lana. It was something he would eventually have to deal with, but now was not the time.

"I like Lana, and I know that Maggie couldn't be any more loved or cared for then she is with her." The social worker removed her glasses and rubbed at her eyes. "But it's my job and the judge's job to make sure that everyone's interest in the child is explored and taken into consideration. Having said that, I'm going to admit that right now I feel the best place for Maggie is still with Lana."

Well, she couldn't be any more honest than that, thought Trent. And what kind of argument did he have to use against her?

"That doesn't mean you won't win custody," she continued. "As a family member, you have a strong case. Your biggest job is going to be to prepare yourself to take on everything raising your niece will require, and it's not going to be easy. I'm not sure you're ready for this change in your life. As a pediatrician, I'm sure you know there's more to raising a child than just providing for their needs."

Was she right? Was he fooling himself, thinking he could take on the job of raising a toddler? And this was adorable little Maggie, who had already been through so much in her short life. The last thing she needed was for him to do something that could screw her up.

Just look what had happened to Michael. He had been supposed to take care of him. He had been the oldest and he'd known his mother expected him to look out for his little brother. He had failed Michael and he didn't want to fail his niece too. But no matter what Lana and the social worker thought Maggie needed him. He was the only one who would be able to protect her from his father's control.

Trent quickly agreed to the home visit the state required before leaving the social worker's office. He had a lot to think about after this meeting.

Lana should have felt at least a little bit of guilt about what she was about to do to Trent, but she didn't. The idea had come to her in the middle of the night, when thoughts of losing Maggie had kept her awake.

While Trent talked a good game as far as wanting to be a responsible uncle and taking on the duty of caring for his niece went, in truth he had no idea of what taking care of Maggie would entail. Sure, he was qualified as a pediatrician to give proper medical care to a child, but she was pretty sure he wasn't really prepared for the day-to-day care a toddler needed.

An early call to Emily, the midwife covering deliveries this weekend, and everything had been set up. The fact that Maggie had woken up cranky from the teeth she was cutting was just the icing on the cake.

"I'm so sorry about this," she said to Trent now, trying to keep the evil laugh inside her from exploding, "but I didn't know I was going to have to cover the hospital today, and Amanda is out of town visiting with her parents."

"So, what exactly do I need to do?" Trent asked as he looked down at Maggie, who was still in her sleeper, with a good amount of oatmeal smeared on her face, her nose crusty with the mucus caused by her teething.

"You'll be fine," she said. "I've laid her clothes out in her room, and her lunch and her supper are in the fridge."

"Supper?" he asked.

"You know how deliveries are—some of

them take hours, and there's no way for me to know when I'll get off. But don't worry—I'll be relieved early enough in the morning that you can make your shift tomorrow. You did say you were working Sunday, didn't you?"

"Uh, yeah… Sunday," Trent said.

Had the man's skin paled, or was that just wishful thinking?

"You'll be fine, Trent," she said.

Reaching down to hug her little girl, she took a second to make sure she didn't have a temperature. Maggie had never been one to run a fever while teething, but there was always a first time. She had no doubt that her daughter would be safe with Trent—she just wasn't sure if Trent would survive the day with the cranky toddler.

Trent looked down at the little girl holding on to his leg. Had she just wiped her nose on his jeans? This child, dressed in some kind of one-piece jumper, with food caked on her mouth, looked nothing like the Maggie he knew. Picking her up in his arms, he made another discovery: she smelled worse than she looked. The first order of business would have to be cleaning her up.

After fighting with her to get her face washed, taking off her dirty sleep outfit seemed a breeze. Putting new clothes on his niece was another matter. He tried all the tricks he knew from his practice. The tickle move he used before giving shots, his funny faces for after the shots, the calm voice he had learned to use with stressed-out kids.

Nothing in his box of tricks worked. It seemed the child was a nudist at heart and had no desire to wear any clothes. By the time he'd managed to get a clean diaper and a shirt on her, he gave up the battle. If running around half dressed made the child happy, so be it.

"I surrender to Princess Maggie," he said, then bowed his head to the toddler.

Maggie giggled at him, then ran to get a little plastic and crystal crown that was sitting on a small bookcase. She stopped and looked through the books stacked in piles, then pulled one out, sending the rest of them tumbling to the ground. Walking over to where he sat on the floor, she sat down on his lap and handed him a book.

He looked at the title. “A princess book for a princess?” he said. “I can do this.”

Opening the pink sparkly book, he wasn’t surprised to see a young girl dressed all in pink wearing a crown. He started to read.

Four books later he noticed Maggie’s eyes drooping. Closing the book, he carefully got off the floor, trying not to disturb the sleepy baby. Laying her down in her crib, he tiptoed out of the room and smiled. What had he been so afraid of? Taking care of Maggie was nothing he couldn’t handle.

He had just shut the door when the crying began.

Lana opened the door and stared at the chaos of her living room. Every toy Maggie owned had to be in that room—plus what looked like half the clothes from her dresser. She leaned down to pick up a large stuffed elephant that was in her way, then froze.

Stretched out on her couch was Trent—a sound asleep Trent. He held her sleeping daughter on top of him, with one of his arms laid protectively around her.

While wide-awake Trent, with his powerful

frame and those mesmerizing blue eyes of his, was a seductive temptation even to her, this version of the man took her breath away. Thick, dark lashes lay resting on copper-toned skin, while lips usually turned up in a smile were relaxed in soft invitation.

She'd felt those lips against hers. She bent down closer. Had they really been that warm? That firm?

Bright blue eyes stared up at her and she jerked away from him. Heaven help her—had she really been about to kiss him? No, of course not. She'd never do anything like that.

"I need to put Maggie down in her crib," she said, trying to keep her voice even while her heart tried to come out of her chest.

Lifting Maggie up into her arms, she held her tight against her racing heart as she carried her into her room and laid her in her crib. She took a minute to catch her breath, then walked back into the living room where she found Trent sitting up and rubbing the back of his neck.

"I can't believe you did that," he said.

"What?" she said. Her heart sped up. Had he caught her?

"You got her to stay in her crib," he said.

She watched him walk toward the door, shoulders slumped and feet all but dragging, and said a silent thank-you to the sleeping Maggie.

"Just one of those tricks you learn when you're a mother," she said.

"You're a good mother, Lana," he said. "I just want you to know that. This isn't about me not thinking you can take care of Maggie."

"Then *what*, Trent? What *is* it about if not what's best for Maggie?"

She stilled as Trent's hand came up to her face. He ran the back of his hand down one cheek, then cupped her chin. He pulled her to him and laid on her lips a kiss so soft that she wondered if she'd imagined it.

He pulled away, a half-smile on his lips, and walked out the door.

As the door shut behind him she took a deep breath and let her body relax. From what she had seen she'd have to say that operation Teach Trent a Lesson about Parenthood had been a success—but would it be enough?

She still had so many unanswered questions. She knew that Trent's guilt concerning his brother's death was part of what was driving him to seek custody of Maggie, but she couldn't help but think there was something he was keeping from her—something important that would explain everything.

Trent sat in his car and watched as other employees came and went from the staff entrance to the hospital. So it all was about to hit the fan. The text he'd received from his lawyer that morning had been short, but to the point.

He looked down to read it one more time.

Time running out. Getting pressure. Must address other parts of your brother's will which includes your father. Will is set to go into probate this week.

His plan had been so simple. Go to Florida. Get child. Protect child from his father. Show the old man that he didn't have the power to control everyone's life anymore. So simple—and yet it had turned so complicated. And that complication was named Lana. Watching her interact with his niece had changed everything.

He never should have come here. He should have stayed far away from both Maggie and Lana and had his lawyer handle everything.

But it was too late. He had got involved and now he had to take control of the situation.

He knew his next move should be to have his lawyer start applying pressure to the courts to get this thing done, but he had been dragging his feet. He was normally a very decisive man, but suddenly he couldn't determine a plan of action that he felt comfortable with.

His knew his father would be on this before he even left the probate hearing. He needed to come up with a new plan. One that was sure to protect his niece. And although he had ignored the social worker's earlier comment, about Maggie needing both him *and* Lana, after Ms. Nelson had shared her concerns with him he had caught himself considering her observation.

After taking care of Maggie all by himself, he had to admit that caring for a toddler was going to be harder than he had first considered. Oh, he could hire a nanny to take care of Maggie, but that didn't sit right with him. That wasn't what he wanted for his niece.

Possibilities entered his thoughts and he mentally made notes. Maybe instead of fighting Lana he could find a way for them to work together. With all the force of his father's lawyers about to descend on them, he had to come up with a plan soon. He didn't have just Maggie to consider—he had to protect Lana too.

Getting out of the car and heading in to work, he willed himself to put everything behind him as he walked into the cool air of the hospital. He prided himself in being able to give his patients his complete attention and he wouldn't let anything get in the way of their care and safety. He'd deal with everything else after his shift.

CHAPTER SEVEN

"I WASN'T EXPECTING YOU," Lana said as she entered her office to find her lawyer, Nathan, sitting in one of the three chairs that circled her desk.

It had only been a few days since she and Trent had met with the social worker and she really hadn't expected to hear any news for at least another week.

"Thought I'd stop and see if you wanted to go out to lunch," Nathan said, and then he saw the sandwich she had laid out on her desk. "But I guess you have that covered."

She had planned a quick lunch and then to use an afternoon free of appointments to catch up on her charting. She had been leaving the office as early as possible the last few days, in order to spend every minute possible with Maggie. The number of file entries she needed to make were beginning to pile up and she had to get caught up. Being behind at work was just one more thing to stress over and she had all the stress she needed right now.

"I have a feeling that I'm not going to feel like eating after all," she said, after taking a seat behind her desk.

Nathan's wife had been one of her first patients when she'd begun her midwifery career. But that didn't explain why he'd shown up here instead of calling. Warning bells started going off in her head, making it almost impossible for her to remain in her seat.

"There's no way you came down here just on the off-chance that you might catch me for lunch," she said. "Especially with having to fight through the noon traffic."

Lana forced her hands to relax on her chair and tried to practice the deep breathing from the labor classes she taught. She had found in the last few days that it helped her get through those times when thoughts of losing Maggie started to overwhelm her.

"So, either you have some really good news that you couldn't wait to share with me or you have some really bad news you didn't want to give me over the phone."

"I got a call from Karen Nelson today that I wanted to talk to you about," Nathan said.

"And here comes the really bad news, I take it?" She sat up straight and braced herself for the blow. "Go ahead. I can take it."

"She's received a call from a lawyer in Houston about Maggie," Nathan said.

She had been wrong. She hadn't been ready for that bombshell at all.

"Trent has hired a new lawyer?" Lana asked.

"No, this one represents Trent's father," Nathan said.

Lana felt the pain of prickling needles shoot through her body as the shock of Nathan's statement hit her. *Maggie's grandfather.* Why hadn't she considered this? Of course the power of two Montgomerys would be stronger than just one. It was taking all she had to fight against one of them—what chance did she have against two of them? How could Trent do this to her?

"Karen Nelson just wanted to give us a heads-up," Nathan said. Leaning over her, he gave Lana a look that would have had her running if she hadn't known he was on her side. "We are going to *fight* this, Lana. I know I told you that we would have a hard time because of Trent's biological relationship, but we still have your history with Maggie. And the fact that the biological mother wanted you to adopt Maggie will play heavily on our side."

"But you know that when one of the biological family requests custody the court usually sides with them. Now there will be two. Two to one, Nathan."

Lana looked down to where her hands now gripped the armrests of her chair. So much for learning to deal with her stress. There was no way she was going to be able to ignore this hit. But Trent should have told her he was going to do this. They had agreed to be honest with each other, hadn't they? Even if there hadn't been any way to talk him out of it, he could have warned her. The fact that he hadn't told her caused an ache deep down inside her chest.

Suddenly, the butterflies that had been in her stomach for the last couple of weeks stopped doing jumping jacks. Now they seemed to have picked up pitchforks and were trying to fight their way out. A wave of nausea rolled over her and she made herself take a deep breath to calm her stomach.

Then a new emotion hit her. A burning anger

boiled up from a stomach that only minutes ago had been ready to spew. How *dared* the man worm his way into her life and then blindside her this way?

The more she thought about it, the madder she got. Maybe it was time for her to show Trent that she was ready for a fight too.

When Nathan had finally quit trying to talk her out of rushing over to Trent's, he called his office and got the address for her. She wouldn't approach him at work, but if she had to hunt him down at his place she would do it.

After promising that she wasn't going to commit murder, she talked her lawyer into leaving the office. She hated it that the poor man would be worrying about needing to have bail posted for her for the rest of the day, but she knew that this was something she had to do.

Even if confronting Trent didn't get her anywhere, at least she'd feel better. She was tired of just sitting back and letting everybody else have a part in deciding her daughter's future. Maggie was *hers* and she wasn't going to just lie down and let somebody come down from Texas and take her child away from her.

She called the hospital and asked for Trent's schedule. Marty, the prenatal technician on duty, seemed suspicious about her needing the information, but with some sweet talk she managed to find out that Trent had gotten called in during the night and had been given the day off in exchange.

Marty was one of the quieter techs in the department, who normally just went about his business, but she would still be surprised if he didn't leak details of her call to the other techs in the department. She could expect a resurgence of gossip by the next time she was on the labor unit, but that was the least of her problems.

She had trusted Trent and he had let her down by pulling this last strategy on her. He needed to know that she wasn't going to be scared off by him and his father. If the Montgomerys wanted a fight she would give them one. What did she have to lose?

Just the most important person in her life—her daughter.

The ride over through bumper-to-bumper traffic just got her more ready for a fight. By the time she pulled up into the driveway of a two-story townhouse she was prepared to confront Trent.

She couldn't believe she had fallen for that sweet Texas drawl of his and let down her guard. Okay, it hadn't been just that sexy accent he had. No, Trent had been blessed with the whole package. From his hard body to his sweet smile. She hadn't had a chance. Had that been the plan all the time? Was he just the front man for his father?

Yeah, the gloves were coming off now and she wasn't going to leave till she got some answers.

When ringing the doorbell didn't get a response she began pounding the decorative knocker on the front door. It didn't get any better results, but it sure did make her feel better. She had become a fountain of adrenaline, and she was about to spill over if she didn't get to burn it off soon.

Finally, she heard the door being unlocked and saw the knob turn. She was ready to blast Trent with everything she had when the door opened.

One look at the man standing in the foyer had

her swallowing her words and forgetting her name. His inky dark hair was bed-tousled and his eyes, heavy with sleep, were seductive and inviting. His chest was bare and she followed the fine line of dark hair down his taut abs until it disappeared under a pair of silk sleeper pants that rode low on his hips and made no secret of the fact that he wore nothing under them.

He could have been born of any of the thousand fantasies that had filled her nights since meeting him. For a second she just stopped and drank him in as she thanked the fates that had seen fit to give her at least this moment of pleasure. How was she supposed to fight with this man when her whole body had suddenly melted into a puddle of need that had to be steaming up his front porch with its heat?

And then she remembered Maggie—sweet little Maggie who needed her so much.

She watched Trent scrub at his jaw as he tried to shake off the remnants of sleep that seemed to be holding him captive. She could almost feel the rough sensation of the bristly stubble as it nuzzled her neck and tickled her chin.

Dreams, she reminded herself, those had just been dreams.

"Lana?" Trent said as he rubbed at his eyes, as if he was trying to get everything awake and operable. "Did I oversleep and miss something?"

"What…?" she said.

"Come in. Let me go change. I'll be right back." Trent said, and then turned to walk into his house.

Lana felt cool air hit her as she walked into the foyer. And after a couple steps into the room she felt herself surface from her lust-induced fog. This would never do. She couldn't keep letting him do this to her.

"Wait," she said as she caught up to him in a large room that opened into a modern stainless steel kitchen and a formal dining and living room. "Nathan told me about your father."

Trent stopped and turned back toward her. Was that remorse she saw in the pained expression on his face? For her? Or was it for himself? Did he regret that she had found out his plan? She wouldn't have known anything about his father's lawyer if the social worker hadn't informed Nathan. Maybe he had planned to throw her off by waiting till the court date to hit her with this news.

"Let me get some clothes on," Trent said, then turned to walk away.

Yeah, clothes. Clothes would be good. Maybe if the man covered up some of that inviting skin of his she would be able to think.

A glance around at the cool white-upholstered couches and off-white carpeting and walls had her imagining the damage one little toddler could do to a room like this. Images of Trent playing tea party with Maggie came to mind, and for a second she imagined a future with the three of them together, sharing lazy Sundays and evenings curled up together on the couch.

She shook her head, forcing the fantasies from her mind. She was happy with her daughter and their little block bungalow with its toy-strewn rooms. They had become a family. *Her* family. She wasn't going to let anyone destroy that. Not Trent and not his father.

But would the court see it the same way? She couldn't compete with all the things Trent and his family could give Maggie. She did okay in her midwife practice, and could certainly provide for Maggie, but looking around the expensively furnished room reminded her of the difference between her life and the Montgomerys'. It was just another thing where the judge could find her lacking.

"Ready to talk?" Trent asked as he walked into the room.

He had changed into a pair of worn jeans and a pale blue tee shirt but he'd left his feet bare, which gave him a casual look that did nothing to squash the desire she had felt for him earlier. She stared down at the long toes peeking out from the hem of his jeans. Who knew bare feet could be so sexy?

Lana shook her head. She was lusting after his toes? *Toes?* Someone really needed to come up with a vaccine she could take to keep her safe from this man. She had to snap out of it. She had to get back in control of herself. She had to get some answers.

"So what was the plan, Trent? Come to Florida and play nice with the little midwife while your father was back home putting together a legal team to fight me?" Lana asked.

The anger that had spurred her into hunting down Trent had died somewhere between his opening the door and her walking into the house. She was so tired of playing games with him. Why couldn't he just be up-front with her? Didn't she deserve that?

He dropped his eyes for a minute, and then looked up as he rubbed the back of his neck. He looked more like a sheepish kid who had gotten caught with his hand in the cookie jar then a man who was trying to tear her world apart. How did he break her heart one minute and then rev it up the next? She felt as if she was being pulled in two when she was around him and she just couldn't keep going like this. Something had to give—and soon.

"I was going to call you and explain to you today..." Trent started. He ran his hands through his hair, then held them out to her. "Look... It's not what you think. I've tried to keep my father out of this. If anything, I've been trying to keep him out of Maggie's life—and yours."

"I don't understand," Lana said.

"Come sit down," Trent said as he reached for her hand.

She looked at the hand he held out to her. Another ploy? But one look at him had her doubting her earlier suspicions. He was pulling off the performance of his life ifthe pain she saw in his eyes was just an act. She knew better than to trust him, but still…

Trent sat, then pulled Lana down next to him. The warmth of her body eased the coldness that seeped into him whenever he had to deal with his old man. Her rigid posture told him she still didn't trust him. And could he blame her?

How much to tell her? He had to gain back her trust if there was any way for them to move on and do the right thing for his niece. She would need to be prepared for the force of his father's influence.

He had no doubt his father would be pulling out all the stops now that he knew the conditions of Michael's will. Would she even understand what his father was like when it came to the family company? Of course it was more of an empire now. He had to give that to his father. The man had taken the small-time oil company his mother had inherited and made a multi-billion-dollar business out of it.

But how did he explain the dysfunction his father's obsession with the company had caused? He would have to start at the beginning. Digging into his past would be painful, but he had to make her understand what she was up against. What the two of them were up against.

"My parents came from totally different backgrounds. My mother was an only child and, while my grandparents weren't nearly as successful as my father has been with the oil company my Grandfather Lord started, she was well provided for. She went to all the right schools and had everything she wanted."

He felt Lana relax against him and some of the tension in his own body eased. Maybe he would be able to win her trust back. Maybe she would realize he hadn't had any choice other than to try to protect his niece.

"But my dad was a different story. Grandpa Montgomery worked for Grandfather Lord out on the ranch. He worked hard, and he had a wife and four kids. From what I've been told, my dad grew up helping his dad out with ranch chores," he said.

"So your parents grew up together?" Lana asked.

She was so close now that he could feel the vibration when she spoke. It was nice. He wasn't a man usually comfortable with someone in his personal space, but this felt good. Safe.

"Yeah, they did. Eventually they grew up, and I guess they fell in love and married."

"You *guess*?" she asked.

"I don't know. I think they loved each other at first. I do remember some times when I was young when they seemed happy together, but in the end all I remember is their fighting."

And his mother crying. He remembered his mother crying and his dad storming out of the house.

"My uncle has told me that my father buried himself in the business because he needed to prove to himself and the company that he could handle it."

"It couldn't have been easy for him to come into the company that way," said Lana.

"No—knowing where my father came from, I'm sure there were often people making comments about him marrying into the company."

His uncle had said as much on the many times he had taken sides with his brother when Trent had complained about his father ignoring Michael's problems.

"I'm sure it was hard at first, but by the time

my mother died he had doubled the company's size and he should have been able to spare some time for Michael."

"You say Michael—what about you? You were just a boy yourself when your mother passed. Didn't you need a father too?"

"Michael was the youngest. He needed him more."

Trent looked away when Lana responded with a snort.

"You've got to understand… Michael was the baby of the family."

"What you're saying is that he was left to do whatever he wanted and there was no adult there to hold him accountable," she said.

"Unfortunately, yes," Trent agreed. "And it just got worse as he got older. I tried to help him, but he wouldn't listen to me. By the time my father decided to take an interest in him he was already in trouble. That's when things got really bad at home."

"Why?" she asked.

Trent felt his body tense. Talking about his brother was difficult, but it had to be done.

"Michael got into some trouble with the law and suddenly my father decided he needed to take control of the situation." He hated the bitterness he could hear in his voice. "By that time I had gone off to college and made it plain that I wasn't going to follow in the old man's footsteps. I guess my father knew that his only chance to pass on the company was through Michael."

"And Michael wasn't interested?"

"No, actually, just the opposite. For a while it looked like he was going to straighten out his life. But it seemed the harder he tried the more my father wanted from him. I think eventually he just gave up."

"What happened to Michael, Trent?"

"It was just too much for him. He started playing around with drugs. Street drugs, prescription drugs… I think he tried them all. Before I knew it he was hooked. We sent him to the best rehabs in the country, but in the end the drugs won. One night he just took too many and that was the end."

"Was it an accident or…?" Lana reached over and wrapped her arms around him.

"I don't know." But, God, how he hoped it had been an accident. Losing his brother to drugs had torn him up inside. Thinking that his brother had ended his own life was more than he could bear.

"I'm so sorry that you lost Michael, but what does this have to do with me and Maggie?"

"My father likes to take control of situations. It's what he did with my brother—what he tried to do with my mother. He'll want to take over Maggie's life too. He's powerful, Lana. He has the means to take Maggie away from you and I'm afraid he won't be satisfied until he does."

Trent felt tears on his shoulder where she had laid her head. He knew the tears were as much for him as they were for her. That was his Lana. She had a big heart. One that she had opened up to a young mother and a little baby. And now he was tearing her heart out when he should be thanking her for taking that little baby in and giving her a home.

Turning, he hugged her close to him, then slipped his hand under her chin. He began wiping his thumb across the smoothness of her wet cheek and then replaced her tears with soft kisses that led down to her mouth. Taking small sips of her lips, he worked to draw her out of her sorrow. It tore him apart to see her hurting.

"I'm sorry too," he whispered into her mouth. "I'm so sorry."

"Then show me," she whispered as she began kissing him back. "Take away the pain…make it all go away."

Lana let go of the hurt and the worry and gave in to her body's demands. Somehow it had separated her desire for Trent from her fear. She needed to forget all the pain, all the fear that haunted her every second of every day. She needed him to satisfy this ache, this itch, this all-consuming desire he made her feel that left her waking each night tangled in her sheets, frustrated and hurting.

She always did the right thing, the safe thing. Just for once she wanted to be able to do what she wanted without worrying about the consequences. To let go of all the reasons this was wrong and allow herself the freedom to just enjoy the moment.

She plunged into him.

Pleasure coursed through her at the feel of his hot, wet mouth. He tasted of spicy mint, and as his tongue circled hers she let the last remnants of anger leave her body. There was nothing to hold her back now. She combed her hands through his thick curls, then tightened her grip to anchor his lips against hers.

His hands stroked up and down her back in a rhythm that matched the mating of their tongues. He deepened his kiss, then ran his hands lower until they cupped her butt and lifted her up over him. She felt him long and hard against her belly and her body answered his with a wet need that pooled between her legs.

“Ah, Lana…” he groaned as he pulled back.

She reached for the bottom of his shirt, then ran her hands up inside till she found his nipples. She let her thumbs caress the twin nubs till they puckered for her. She felt his hands undo the clasp of her bra, then circle back around to her freed breasts. Her breath caught inside her when she felt him cup their weight. The feel of his coarse hands against her nipples had her arching into him. She’d wanted this—no, *needed* this since that first kiss in the locker room.

She let her hands trail lower as they followed the soft line of hair down his chest. The feel of his abs tightening at her touch urged her on to her target. She felt him tense, heard him moan as she teased the skin along his waistband. For the first time in her life she felt power in love-making and it was exhilarating. Trent made her feel like a real, whole woman—not broken like Joe had made her feel.

Yes, Trent had been with more experienced women then her—women who would have known how to attract and satisfy him—but there wasn't any way that a woman had ever wanted him more than she did at that moment. Maybe she had never learned the art of seduction, but she wasn't going to let her old insecurities stop her. She was too far gone now. No way was she going to let her feelings of inadequacy spoil this. No more waiting for what she wanted. She would take it this time.

Surprising herself, she let her hand wander down to his fly, where she let her nails run up and down over the teeth of the zipper. Feeling the hard ridge beneath the clothing, she teased herself as much as him—until she could no longer stand the thought of being this close yet still not touching him. She undid the button of his jeans and eased the zipper down.

* * *

Feeling the pressure ease as Lana lowered the zipper of his jeans, Trent fought for control. Backing away, he grabbed her hand, stilling its motion while at the same time pressing it against the length of him. Resting his head against her forehead, he took a deep breath… and then another. He needed to gain control or he would end up taking her on the floor where they stood.

What was it about her that heated his blood so hot that he couldn't think when she was around? As she closed her hand around him his whole body tensed with a need he had never known before. This woman, with her pure heart and sweet curvaceous body, undid him. If he didn't get her hands off him right then it would all be over. His body was going to go up in flames any minute.

He removed her hand and held it tightly in his own. They had to slow down. He nceded to think.

Looking down into her wild green eyes, he was amazed by the trust he saw there. She was amazing in her capacity to love and nurture. It was unlike anything he had ever seen or known. The thought of being the one who was able to gift her with what she needed right then humbled him. He felt his own need as it pounded into his heart. He knew he wasn't worthy of the honor, but he felt no shame in his desire for her. Maybe in this one thing they could come together and give each other the comfort they both needed right now.

Keeping his eyes connected with hers, he threaded his fingers through hers and drew her up from the couch. He led her down the hall into his bedroom, where there would be no one but him and her, choosing to grab this precious time for themselves. He had to do this right. Things were so complicated between them now and he couldn't mess this up.

He shut the door behind them and turned to her.

"We leave everything, everybody, on the other side of that door. Can you do that, Lana?" he asked as he closed the space between them.

Lana forced herself to concentrate on his words. There would be no going back from here.

Sex had never been something she took lightly, but she had spent the last two years feeling like only half a woman, and she didn't want to feel like that anymore. She knew the intimacy of this moment would change her, touch her deep down in places she had kept guarded since Joe, but she knew it would be worth it.

Sometimes you just had to trust blindly. There could be no love without trust.

Love? Was she that far gone?

Fear suddenly flamed inside her at the thought of loving Trent, but then she remembered his words. He had told her to leave everything outside the door for just these few moments they had together. Could she? Should she?

"Yes," she heard herself say.

No matter how much her brain questioned the insanity of this, there was no other option for her. Both her body and her heart needed him. Right then, right there.

He led her over to his rumpled bed and she watched his face as she released his hand and backed up toward the bed, removing her shirt and letting it fall to the floor, following it with her bra and skirt.

As the afternoon sunlight filtered through the closed blinds she stood there in only a white cotton thong. She should have felt cold and exposed, but as Trent walked towards her she felt the warmth of his eyes as they covered her body. She reached for his hand and led him with her to the bed.

When his arms circled her she let all her misgivings go. She pulled him down and then his hands were everywhere as they stroked and kissed. She let herself explore his arms and chest as she returned his burning kisses, reaching lower until she was circling him with her hands. She thrilled at the hard length that proved his desire for her.

His hands came between them and he began stroking her. She spread her legs to welcome him. Sensations flooded through her as her hips rocked against the thick hard length of him. And then he was there, thrusting inside her with a rhythm she fought to match until she was drenched with sweat.

He arched and stiffened inside her as his body rushed to its climax. Then he reached between them once again and with one shattering stroke she joined him.

Everything around them flew away as they held on to each other. For a brief second she felt them suspended in time, where nothing existed except for the two of them. And then they were crashing back down—together.

Lana glanced at the alarm clock sitting on the nightstand. She would have to leave soon. Amanda had a night class so she would have to pick up Maggie at daycare. She looked across the room, taking in the same simple white color scheme that had been present in what she had seen of the rest of the house.

There was nothing in the room that hinted of Trent's personal taste. White walls, off-white carpet, even shabby-chic white furniture throughout the room. The only thing with any color was the natural oak window trim and the door. The door that kept the world away…the door that allowed them to escape from all the reasons why they shouldn't be here, together, right now.

Wasn't that what everyone had to do sometimes? Just shut everything out and escape into a world where they felt secure and safe, away from all their troubles and free of all their responsibilities, even if it was just for a short time? Was it so bad that they had grabbed this little bit of time for themselves?

She thought of her agreement with Trent. *Leave everything, everybody, on the other side of that door.* But what happened when the door opened? When once again they found themselves in the heated fight that was turning them both inside out? What happened when they both had to face the fact that they were on opposite sides in a battle that had the highest stakes possible and that only one of them could win?

"Shh..." Trent said, and he shifted and drew her closer, trailing his hands through her hair, soothing her with his touch.

Letting go of a breath she hadn't known she was holding, she snuggled down into him. Resting her head on his chest and listening to the steady beat of his heart, she let her body recede into that calm place where Trent had taken her.

She just needed a few more minutes to enjoy the feel of him. Enough time for her to capture this memory. She would wrap it up and take it with her. And when things got bad she would take it out and it would remind her that at least she'd had this moment. This little bit of time when life had been right between the two of them.

* * *

Trent combed his hands through the thick blond mass of hair that lay across his chest, then bent his head and took a deep breath. The soft scent of honeysuckle filled him, making him smile. It was a scent that he had come to recognize as Lana. It was fresh and feminine, with a touch of sweetness that was guileless in its simplicity and so like Lana, who had no desire to be anything but herself.

He had always enjoyed the smell of the little yellow flowers that grew wild on the rickety old fence that lined the entrance to the ranch. Though he could remember many an argument between his dad and mom about the trailing plants, with his dad calling them weeds and fussing about having to clear them every year after they'd died out. But his mom would always just ignore his dad and go right on picking the vines and sticking them into the old Mason jar that she'd kept sitting on the kitchen window sill.

Things were different around the ranch now, but the same old fence still stood, and every year the honeysuckle would grow back. He'd caught his dad staring out the window and looking at the fragrant yellow flowers once, and wondered if possibly the old man was thinking about the wife he had lost.

"I was eight and Michael only four when my mother left and never came back."

He felt Lana turn to him, but he knew he couldn't look down at her. He had promised her that they would keep everything out of the bedroom, but he could fill the world creeping in and knew they would soon have to return to their separate lives.

"She just walked out on you?"

"No. Well, not exactly," he said.

Once more he pulled her up close to him and turned her so that he could rest his chin on the top of her head. He let the scent of her soothe the raw hurt he felt every time he thought of that night twenty-four years ago.

"Mom and Dad had had a bad fight that day. He'd found where she'd hidden her whiskey bottle and had thrown it out the back door. She'd screamed at him about going through her things and he'd hollered back that she had promised to quit drinking. That she had promised there wouldn't be any more alcohol around the house. Then she started crying and telling him that he didn't understand. It was the same argument that they had almost daily. They argued about him always being at work and her always being left alone, but this time it was worse.

"Dad told Mom he'd have her put in a rehab clinic if she didn't stop drinking, and that's when my mom threatened to take the company away from him. My dad finally walked out and I thought things would be okay. That he'd come back in a little while and Momma would tell him that she was sorry and beg him to forgive her. Say that she'd try harder. It was how all their fights ended. They'd hug and kiss and everything would go on just fine."

Trent stopped. He had forgotten about those times when they had made up—the times when they had disappeared for an hour or two alone. Had they been happy together then?

"Your mother was an alcoholic," Lana stated.

"Yes. Looking back now, I can see all the signs. All the times she slept through the day, never getting up to check on either me or Michael. Then there were the times when I would find her hugging the toilet, too sick to hold her head up."

"But you couldn't have known what was wrong with her then. You were just a child," Lana said.

Trent clasped the hand she'd entangled with his. He hadn't really ever talked about that night with anyone. Not even Michael, who had been way too young to understand what was happening at the time.

"No, I didn't know what was wrong—but I did know something wasn't right," he said. "And that day when Momma left us home alone I knew she shouldn't have gone. I knew that moms didn't go off and leave their kids all alone like that. And when it got to be dark and she still hadn't come home, and Michael started crying that he was scared and wanted his momma, I got real mad. I got mad at the both of them."

He'd been scared too. Scared that his parents had both gone off and forgotten about them. But he hadn't told Michael he was scared. He'd had to be strong and take care of Michael.

"Momma said she'd be right back. She was going to run to the store and then she'd be right back. She said that I needed to take care of my little brother because I was the oldest, but that she wouldn't be long. Just a few minutes… that's all it would take her."

Trent remembered how relieved he'd been when he'd seen the lights from his dad's rusted old pick-up pull into the drive. But then his dad had found out that their mom wasn't home and that she'd left them all alone. He'd never seen his dad so mad. He'd been scared all over again. He'd tried to tell his dad that Momma had just gone to the store and that she'd be right back.

Then Harry from the sheriff's office had driven up. He'd seen his daddy shake his head as tears ran down his weathered face.

That was the last time he'd seen his dad show any type of emotion for anything except his damn oil company. His father hadn't even cried at Michael's funeral—but then neither had he. Just how much like his father *was* he?

"Something happened to her, didn't it?" Lana asked in a voice that could barely be called a whisper.

"They found her car where she hit a tree, but I found out later—when I was older—that she had been thrown out of it," Trent said. "The accident report said that they found an open bottle of Jack Daniels on the seat."

* * *

For a few minutes they just lay there in silence as they held each other. Lana couldn't imagine what it had been like for the two little boys, all alone and scared one minute, while they waited for their momma to come home, and then the next to be told she was never coming back.

They'd both been so young, and there was no doubt that they'd been affected by the events of that night. Even Michael, at four, had to have known that their mom was supposed to *be* there. That she was supposed to take care of them. And her asking Trent to watch his brother so that she could go out and buy alcohol had been so irresponsible that it made her wonder if there had been other times when she had put the bottle before her two little boys.

"After my mom died and my great-aunt came to live with us my father devoted all his time to the oil company. Before long it had grown to one of the largest in the state," he said. "That's when he really changed."

Lana felt his hand under her chin, strong but tender as he raised her head up to his.

"The company was the center of his life. It became impossible to please him. No matter what Michael or I did, it was never good enough. By the time I started applying to colleges I knew that I didn't want to be involved with the family business, so I decided to go into medicine. My father has never forgiven me for that decision. He doesn't like it when things don't go his way."

He was *warning* her about his father. "You're not involved with him against me in the custody battle, are you?" she asked.

"No, I'm not," he said. "And now you know all my family's dirty secrets."

A chill washed over her. "We all have secrets," she said, pulling the sheet up higher.

"And you, Lana? Do you have secrets?" he asked.

The outside world was starting to seep into the room and none of it was pretty. He had shared so much with her. Was it not right that she did the same with him? Where things would go between them after this she didn't know, but she knew she needed to be honest about everything with him.

"I need to tell you something," she said, then swallowed.

She felt the slightest tightening of his muscles against her skin.

"Okay," he said.

He settled back in the bed, curling himself around her and pulling her against him, as if protecting her. If only he could… But there were some hurts that even Prince Charming, or in this case a sexy cowboy doctor, couldn't fix.

"When I was sixteen I went to my pediatrician for a school physical and he found a cancerous mass in my abdomen. I was lucky they found it early, but the chemo and radiation…" She took a deep breath, reaching for the strength she needed. "They damaged my ovaries. I can never have children, Trent."

They lay there with nothing but silence between them for a minute, Trent still wrapped around her.

"I'm so sorry, Lana," Trent said. "Cancer is such a harsh disease, and you were so young."

She shrugged her shoulders and pushed herself up, pulling herself away from him. The last thing she wanted Trent to feel for her was pity.

"It was a long time ago. I just thought you should know."

She needed to leave.

She wiped the tears away from her face and reached for the alarm clock to bring it closer to her. Propped up against a crystal lamp was a small picture of her and Maggie as they played in the sand on their trip to the beach. She hadn't known he was taking it—which was a good thing. With her hair soaking wet from their dip in the cold salt water and her face bare of everything except the red hint of sun on the tip of her nose, it was not a good picture of her.

Of course he had been taking pictures of Maggie that day—she had probably just happened to be in this one. But the fact that he had it there, where he would see it every night before he went to sleep, helped ease the pain of knowing that she would never be in this bedroom, behind this door, again.

"I've got to go pick up Maggie," she said as she climbed out of the bed.

Her body immediately felt cold, and she knew it had nothing to do with the air-conditioning in the house. All the warmth that had comforted her earlier was now gone.

She picked up her clothes from where they had been dropped earlier and told herself that everything would be okay between them. They were adults. They had both agreed to keep this time separate from everything else in their life and they would do it. Knowing what she did now about Trent and his father's relationship, there was no doubt that the two of them weren't working together against her, but that still didn't make him an ally. They were still on opposite sides of what was best for Maggie.

"Lana, I'm sorry. About everything. I'm *so* sorry."

Looking back at him, she saw pain in his eyes. And as she left to go back into the world outside she knew that somehow nothing and yet everything had changed since she had walked inside that bedroom.

Trent watched as Lana left the room. His heart went out to the sixteen-year-old girl who had been through so much and then had so much taken away from her after surviving cancer. He had seen the pain that still haunted her eyes when she'd talked about not being able to have children.

Looking over at the picture he had placed on the nightstand, he was hit with how unfair it was that the beautiful woman in the photo, who had so much love to give, and who had helped so many women as they labored to bring their children into the world, would never know what it was like to bring her own child into the world.

And as he turned over in his bed he was hit with the realization that his bed felt cold and empty without her.

CHAPTER EIGHT

IT HAD BEEN two days and thirteen hours since she had walked out of Trent's home. She had been waiting for him to contact her. She'd believed him when he'd said he wasn't involved with his father's plans, but she knew there was something going on between him and his father that he was holding back from her. There was a bitterness in Trent's voice whenever he spoke of his father that was inconsistent with everything else she thought she knew about him.

She decided to stop by Labor and Delivery after rounding on her patients on the recovery floor, hoping not only to see him, but also to talk to the charge nurse about the gossip Amanda had heard earlier that week, concerning her and Trent. She needed to address some of the tongue-wagging that was going around the hospital. She could have approached the people she thought were spreading the stories around, but she felt it would be better to have the charge nurse remind them to watch what they were saying.

Arriving on the unit, she found the nurses' station empty, which was never a good sign. Recognizing the flashing emergency light that was going off over Labor Room Five, she sprinted down the hall.

"Lana, we need some help," said Laurie, who was the day charge, as soon as she saw Lana enter the room.

Lana recognized the two nurses who were trying to strip the clothes off a pale woman whose rounded belly indicated that she was due at any time.

"What do you need me to do?" Lana offered as she approached the bed.

The metallic smell hit her before she saw the blood that pooled between the patient's legs. The young woman looked to be of Asian descent and she seemed to be pleading in a language that Lana couldn't understand.

"What's she saying?" she asked as she grabbed the heart monitor and applied it to the swollen belly.

"Save my baby," said the man standing at the

other side of the bed, holding her hand. "She doesn't want to lose our baby."

Lana touched the woman's abdomen and felt the hard tone of the uterus. Looking further down, she saw the outline of a faded scar. "Did she have surgery when she had another baby?" she asked the man.

"Yes—with our three sons. She was supposed to have another C-section."

"Ruptured uterus?" Laurie asked as she passed her a small hand-held ultrasound.

"No, I think her placenta is abrupting," Lana said as she looked at the black and white screen.

The labor monitors started to beep and the fetal heartbeat began tracing across the screen. It was lower than normal, but if they got the baby out fast it would have a chance.

The blood pressure machine went off too, and the cuff on one of the patient's arms began to tighten.

"Who's the doctor on call?" Lana asked as they worked to turn the patient and remove the rest of her clothes.

"Dr. Bradley and he's on his way," Laurie said. "We've already called the nursery and Dr. Montgomery is on his way over too."

The charge nurse finished inserting an intravenous needle and hung a large bag of fluids to help replace some of the volume of blood the patient was losing.

"We need to get her to the operating room *now*," Lana said as she looked at the low blood pressure reading that flashed up on the monitor. "I'll assist. Where's anesthesia?"

"Right here," said Debra, the nurse anesthetist, as she walked into the room. She grabbed a pair of gloves on her way to the bed when she saw the blood that was quickly filling the clean pads they'd just applied.

"Okay, let's roll," the charge nurse ordered her staff.

While Debra rushed to get her equipment ready, Lana stopped to put her arm around the father of the baby. She walked him out to the small waiting room outside the operating theater. The man had begun to tremble the minute he had left his wife's side and she knew he needed to sit down.

Lana was very familiar with the feeling of helplessness that the man had to be feeling, with both his wife and his child's life in danger. Bending down so that they were on eye level, she took his hand and gave it a squeeze. "What's her name?" Lana asked.

"Joy. Her name is Joy," he said.

"Is she allergic to anything that you know of?" she asked.

"No," he answered, then looked up at her with dark troubled eyes. "Will she be okay?"

"We're going to take good care of her," Lana said, then rose to her feet and headed for the door. "I'll let you know any news as soon as I can."

"And the baby? Will the baby be okay?" she heard him ask as she was leaving the room.

She wanted to ignore the question, knowing that her answer wouldn't bring the relief that this father wanted, but that was the cowardly way out and what he needed was honesty. He needed to be prepared in case the worst happened.

"I don't know," she answered quietly, then turned and headed for the scrub sink.

The operating room would have appeared to be in chaos to anyone who didn't know that every one of the staff members there was competently doing their job. As she dried her hands on the sterile towel one of the techs handed her, Lana turned in a circle so that one of the nurses could tie her up in a sterile gown.

Checking the fetal monitors, she saw that the fetal heart tones, which had been dipping down with the contractions earlier, were remaining low. They needed to hurry and get the baby out—but they had no choice but to wait for the surgeon.

She looked over as the swinging doors opened and Trent walked in with the neonatal team. They went straight over to the warmer unit and began setting up the resuscitation equipment. They had already opened the crash cart so that they would be ready as soon as the baby was handed to them. This was a situation where a few wasted seconds could be a matter of life or death.

"What do we have?" Trent asked as he moved over to her.

She had thought she would be uncomfortable the next time she saw Trent after their afternoon together, but right now all she felt was relief at the sight of him. If there was anything that could be done for this baby when they delivered it she knew Trent would do it.

"Patient's name is Joy. Past C-section times three…placenta abruption on arrival. She doesn't speak much English," she said.

She watched as he moved over to the neonatal team and started giving orders. And the whole time, as people turned the woman from side to side, stuck monitor pads on her arms and chest and applied all the necessary monitors, she kept pleading with that sad voice for her child's life.

"Is everyone ready?" asked Dr. Bradley as he entered the OR and reached for a sterile towel to dry his hands.

Lana's breath came a little easier at the sight of the OB doctor entering the room. As the circulating nurse reviewed the patient's history and her presentation at the hospital he gowned and gloved. He called for the patient's name and then did a time-out, to assure everyone was aware of the procedure and the patient.

While everyone in the room listened to Laurie's report the staff positioned the instruments where they could easily be handed to the doctor. Debra from Anesthesia was injected some medicine into Joy's IV and then inserted the endotracheal tube, so that she would be able to control her breathing while she was under anesthesia.

Seconds after the team was in position Dr. Bradley made an incision into the abdomen. Lana operated the suction, trying to clear all the blood and fluid so that the doctor could see as he made his way through to the uterus. He cut into the uterus and removed a pale, still baby girl.

Lana remembered that Joy's husband had said they had three boys at home. This mother must be so excited about having a little girl. Lana felt the mask that covered her nose and mouth become damp as she watched Trent and the neonatal team begin to work on the quiet baby.

"We're not finished here, people," Dr. Bradley said, getting back the attention of his team. "Let them work on the baby. Our job is to fix this momma."

Lana quickly returned her attention to assisting while the doctor delivered the placenta and then repaired the uterus and closed the incision. Meanwhile Trent had quickly intubated the small baby and was working on getting intravenous access.

Finally the doctor closed the last layer of the earlier incision and the staff could relax.

"I have to go check on the staff," Laurie said as she pulled off her mask. "Melody, you take over here."

"I've got her," the nurse responded.

Lana moved over next to Trent as he finished putting a line through the umbilical cord. One of the respiratory team continued to bag the baby, but her color was still a dusky blue.

"Will she make it?" she asked him.

"I don't know," he answered. "Her heartbeat is still a little slow, but we've ordered blood to transfuse. The sooner we can get that in her the better."

A shrill alarm sounded and Trent quickly turned back as the monitor showed the baby's oxygen saturation falling rapidly.

"Rate?" he asked the nurse who was listening to the baby's heart with a stethoscope.

"Fifty-six," she answered.

"Start compressions," he ordered. "Where's that blood?"

"It's on its way up from the lab," another nurse said. "I'm drawing up the epinephrine now."

"Go ahead and give it," he said.

Lana watched as yet another nurse walked in with a small packet of blood and began setting up the tubing. She waited as all the nurses co-ordinated their compressions and ventilations, feeling helpless but knowing there was nothing she could do but pray for a miracle.

"Pulse-check," Trent ordered.

"One hundred and twenty," said the nurse checking the pulse.

"Let's go," he said to the team, and they rushed out with the new baby.

Lana looked down at the blood on her scrubs. Unless she wanted to give her staff and her patients a scare, she would need a new pair before she went back to her office.

She pulled out her beeper and was surprised to find that it had only been thirty minutes since she had walked onto the unit. It always felt so much longer when you knew there was a life depending on your speedy response.

Lana was just stepping out of the locker room when Trent walked in. He couldn't get his thoughts off the woman who had been on the operating table. He knew that she would be physically okay once she got into Recovery. It was the woman's emotional reaction to hearing that her baby was in critical condition that would affect the young mother the most.

Would she be able to cope if her baby didn't make it? What about Lana? Would *she* be able to cope if she lost Maggie?

It was thoughts of Lana that had sent him here, looking for her.

"The baby?" she asked when she saw him.

"Now that we've got a transfusion going her color is better, but it's too soon to know how she'll do. I just wanted to grab some new scrubs," he said.

"'Save my baby. Don't let me lose my baby,'" Lana quoted as she leaned against the locker room wall. "She kept telling us that. And I can't lose *my* baby, Trent. I can't lose Maggie."

He felt his heart break when Lana looked up at him, her eyes brimming with tears.

"Don't, Lana…" he said as he came over and put his arms around her. Pulling her down to the closest bench, he rubbed his hands up and down her arms, where goosebumps peppered her skin.

"I don't know if I'm crying for her or for me," Lana said as she wiped away her tears with the back of her hands. "Selfish, huh? To be thinking about myself when that poor woman doesn't know if her baby is going to live or die?"

Trent moved her hands out of the way, then used the pads of his own thumbs to wipe at her tears. How could she ask that? She was the most unselfish person he had ever met.

He had watched her with her patients. She could be falling-down tired, but she remained at their side no matter how long they needed her. She thought of everybody's needs—even his—before herself. She only asked for one thing for herself. To be able to raise the little girl she had taken into her heart.

"No, I don't think you're selfish. I'm surprised you haven't broken down before now," Trent said as he held her face between his hands. "Look at me," he said when she tried to look away. "I came here without any thought of how it would affect anyone except me. But I think I have a way to make things right—to fix this. But I need a few more days to work things out."

"I stopped by to see her husband. He says the baby's name is Hope."

Trent looked down into those pure green eyes

that swam with tears. There was hope there now. He couldn't let her down. A hint of doubt sparked through him. He had let Michael down, hadn't he? How could he know that he wouldn't fail Lana too?

"I've got to get back," Trent said, then pulled away from her.

As he opened the door he looked to where she sat on the old wooden bench. She was bent over, with her elbows resting on her knees and her beautiful blond hair falling around her face, staring down at the dull gray carpet on the floor. He was doing the right thing—the only thing he *could* do right now. But that didn't mean it was over. He would find a way to work this out. He just had to.

He had no doubt that she would agree to anything to keep his niece, but his plan would come at a cost for both of them. He felt the weight of guilt hit him at his thoughts of sacrifice. He should tell her about the stipulations of the will. But would she understand how important it was for him to be able to protect Maggie from his father's influence? Or would he lose the trust he'd just seen in her eyes?

He walked back into the nursery with new

determination as he remembered Lana's face as she had looked up at him, with all her faith in him in her eyes. She trusted him, and the weight of that trust lay heavy on him.

He wouldn't let her down. This time he would protect those who were depending on him. He couldn't fail Lana and Maggie.

"Of course I understand that you want to know your granddaughter, Father."

Trent tried to relax his grip on the phone. He was getting nowhere fast in this conversation. But he had enough experience in dealing with his father that he knew not to push at this point. He'd let the man try to convince him that this was all about family. As if Calvin Montgomery knew *anything* about family…

Trent had been thinking a lot about his childhood since his talk with Lana. There had been times when he was young when his father had spent time with him and his brother. It had been his father who had taught him to ride his first horse. And there had been a few fishing and camping trips with the whole family together. He would have sworn that his parents had been happy then—would have sworn that his father had truly cared about his sons.

But things had changed when his mom had passed away. It had been as if his father had just given up on his family after that. They'd all been damaged, with his father devoting more and more of his time to the business and Michael getting into more and more trouble. And Trent had found himself hiding behind his school work and spending as much time at his uncle's house as possible.

Hitting the "end call" button on his phone as soon as his father had ended their conversation, he gave himself some credit for not throwing it against the wall. His father reaching out to him like this was just a sign of things to come. He could expect more pressure now that the lawyers would be getting involved. There were too many people fighting over one little innocent girl.

He'd realized the night before, while he was lying in bed, looking at his picture of little Maggie and Lana, that really none of them had taken into account the fact that not only did Lana love Maggie as if she was her own, but Maggie loved Lana too.

That was what Lana had been trying to tell him in the social worker's office, but he hadn't listened. He hadn't wanted to hear what she was saying. But it was there in the picture, where Maggie was smiling up at Lana with all the love in her little heart. What would Maggie think if they took her away from Lana? That her mother had just gone off and left her?

He'd remembered the feeling he'd had when he had realized his mother wasn't coming back. He had been so scared. The thought of Maggie being scared like that had tied his stomach into knots, and he had known he couldn't let anything happen that would leave the child feeling like that.

So he'd woken up this morning and decided to take action to protect both woman and child.

Now, after glancing at his watch, he poured the coffee he'd let get cold while he was talking with his father into the sink. He had half an hour to get to Lana's for his visitation with Maggie and he didn't want to be late. There were plans to be made and action to be taken.

Lana stopped and looked outside her window for the second time in as many minutes. At this rate she would never get anything done. She was in a bad mood today, and it was the irritating man who was supposed to be here at any minute who had her that way. One minute he was all over her—the next he was walking away. A woman could get permanent whiplash, trying to keep up with his coming and going. And what had he meant when he had said he could fix things?

"Maggie, I found your purple puppy!" she called out as she bent down to pick it up off the floor. The toddler was busy pulling out all of her toys, looking for the prized stuffed animal.

She remembered when she had bought the silly-colored toy dog. Maggie had just started to crawl then. She'd been so cute, trying to hold onto her puppy and crawl at the same time. The poor puppy was missing an eye now, and it needed one of its ears to be sewn back on.

She heard a car door slam and felt her body relax. He was here. She hadn't been sure if he would show or not after his cryptic vow to make things right yesterday. She had been afraid that he intended to walk out of her and Maggie's life, and the thought of something that a couple of weeks ago would have thrilled her now left her feeling empty and alone.

She tried to tell herself that the only reason she didn't want Trent to leave was because of Maggie. Her daughter had become very attached to her uncle, and now that she had gotten to know him Lana knew she'd never keep him from seeing his niece.

Taking the stuffed animal into Maggie's room, she glanced at the mirror in the hall. It was a good thing that Amanda had decided to go out shopping with some of her friends today. Her babysitter would have seen right through her if she had seen her primping in front of the mirror.

So maybe she *had* spent a little more time on her make-up than necessary this morning? It certainly wasn't a crime to want to look good when you were doing housework and laundry, was it?

Who was she fooling? It had been years since she had been this concerned about how she looked. Trent had brought out the woman in her—the one that had been dead for the last couple of years. All those feelings of insecurity were almost gone now, and the excitement that filled her at the anticipation of seeing him was new.

She couldn't remember feeling like this even when she had been dating in college. It had to be the absence of a man in her life that was doing this to her. She had been wrong in thinking that since she had given up on marriage she didn't need a man at all. When Trent left she would have to find someone to take his place. She could do that. Couldn't she…?

"Who are you trying to fool? You've got it bad, girl." she said to her reflection, then looked down to see her daughter looking up at her. "Your momma's got to get herself together, Maggie-girl."

She picked the little girl up and gave her a big hug as the doorbell went.

"Now, let's go answer that door and see if we can talk some sense into your Uncle Trent."

She let Maggie greet him first. She couldn't help but smile when he picked her up and she gave him hugs and kisses. Maggie had always been a happy baby, but she had never been so comfortable around a man before. Lana had always blamed it on the fact that she had never been around a man except for Lana's dad, whom Maggie had loved immediately.

"Daddy!" the little girl said as she patted Trent's face with her small hands.

Lana felt the blood leave her face. Maggie had seen other children at daycare being picked up by their dads, so she must have decided that was what all men were called.

Lana reached out and took Maggie from Trent's arms. "I'm so sorry," she said. "I guess she thinks that's what men are called."

"It's no big deal," Trent said as he followed Lana into the house and shut the door behind him. "I've been called a lot of things, but I have to admit that is a first."

Lana looked up at Trent and noticed a tinge of color under his golden tan. Had he been embarrassed by Maggie calling him Daddy? But why? As he'd said, it wasn't a big deal.

"This is your Uncle Trent, Maggie," she told the little girl as she squirmed her way out of her arms.

Maggie immediately went back to Trent and pulled on his jeans leg, asking to be picked up. "Daddy?" she said in her sweet little voice.

"I'm sorry. She must be going through a phase," Lana said.

"It's not a problem, Lana," Trent said as he leaned down to pick the little girl up.

"So, what's the plan for today?" she asked. "Do you just want to hang out here with her or is there something you want to do?"

"I saw a park down the road," he said. "I thought we could go there. The weather is beautiful today, and we can talk while Maggie is playing."

"Let me grab a bag for her," Lana said, and headed down the hall.

So they were back to talking again. She didn't know why they bothered. She wasn't going to change her stand on Maggie's adoption. And he was too tied up with his feelings of being responsible for his brother's actions. They'd just end up chasing the same rabbit down a hole and they'd never come out in the same place together.

Trent watched the two little girls as they played in the sandbox. Even with a fairly small vocabulary the toddlers managed to communicate and play together. Kids were amazing. It was too bad that people seemed to lose that ability when they got older…

He and Lana had been sitting there watching the toddlers for several minutes and he still didn't know how to approach this. Would she go along with his unorthodox plan?

"I thought you wanted to talk?" Lana asked, then turned toward him.

He noticed the way she had pulled back her shoulders, as if she was getting ready for a fight. Well, either that or she was trying to show off the cleavage that was peeking out of the fitted pink tee shirt she was wearing today. He knew if he had to choose between a fight and looking at her breasts, the breasts would win every time.

He tried to smother the laugh he felt coming, but then decided he could use a good chuckle after the week he'd had, so he let go of all the happiness he felt in just this moment and enjoyed it.

"What's so funny?" Lana asked, then looked down to where his eyes were still trained. "Trent Montgomery, are you staring at my breasts? This is not the time!"

Lana had leaned in to whisper, which just gave him a better view.

When she saw his eyes, still peeking down her shirt she laughed herself. "Behave! There are little kids all around us."

He watched Lana tug at the top of her shirt as she pretended to be scandalized by his behavior, but he wasn't fooled. Memories of her in his bed had his body responding in ways that definitely weren't appropriate, considering their location.

He shifted in his seat and crossed his legs so that he wouldn't embarrass her any further.

She peeked over at him from under her thick lashes while she pretended to take in all the people walking and playing in the tree-lined park—though he noticed she didn't let her eyes stray from Maggie for more than a few seconds.

She was such fun to tease, and it was such a beautiful day. He was a lucky man, to be sitting out in the sun with two of the prettiest girls around. Too bad he was going to have to ruin it.

"I talked to my father today," he said.

"Did he mention Maggie?"

"Yes, he did." He stretched out his legs as

he turned toward her. “He fed me some bull about always wanting grandchildren. He even had the nerve to give me a hard time about not having any kids.”

“Why haven’t you?” she asked.

“What?”

“Why haven’t you gotten married? Had children?” she asked. “You know—all the things people normally do by our age?”

Because the thought of living like his father and mother scared the life out of him. He would never be able to live like that. It was better to live alone than to spend his life on a rollercoaster of ups and downs such as his parents had called a marriage.

But maybe, for a little while, he wouldn’t have to be alone. Surely if anyone could manage to make a temporary arrangement work for the security of little Maggie, he and Lana could.

“Why haven’t *you*?” he asked.

“You know why,” she said. “I can’t have children.”

Trent looked over to where Maggie played. “Would it make any difference to how you feel about Maggie if you had given birth to her?” he asked.

He watched her lips curve up in a smile as she watched Maggie playing.

"No, of course not. But it's not that simple," she said, then changed the subject. "What did you mean when you said you could 'fix things,' Trent?"

CHAPTER NINE

LANA WATCHED AS he cleared his throat. She sensed in him the same nervousness that she had felt while discussing her infertility. Was it something so bad that he was scared to tell her?

"I think Ms. Nelson is right. Maggie does need both of us. We need to get married."

The shock of his statement hit her instantly. For a second she thought she would pass out, and then she remembered to breathe. She tried to open her mouth and ask one of the hundreds of questions spinning in her mind, but her voice wouldn't come.

He couldn't be serious. Could he?

"Trent..."

She let him take her hands in his and waited. She had to have misunderstood him.

"Just hear me out, Lana," he said. "Right now we're fighting against each other, when we should be fighting together for what's best for Maggie."

"You know I only want the best for her," she said.

"And with both of us working together we can make sure of that," he said.

"But that doesn't mean we have to get *married*," she said. "This has something to do with your father, doesn't it?"

She couldn't understand what his father could want with her little girl when from what Trent had said he hadn't cared for his own children, but it was plain to see that Trent thought his father was a real threat. Why else would he come up with such a hair-brained idea?

Marriage? To *Trent*?

She fought down a flutter of excitement that wanted to float to the surface. She couldn't let herself get pulled into that happily-ever-after dream again. Marriage was not meant for her. She had gotten her hopes up once, and when Joe had rejected her after he'd learned about her infertility it had nearly destroyed her.

She wouldn't go through that again. Better to accept that her future didn't hold any hope of the traditional family she had always planned on.

"What could be better than the two of us together?" he asked. "We've shown that we can work together and we get along well."

Yes, they did work well together—both in and out of bed—but that wasn't enough to build a marriage on. Was it…?

"And, yes, this has a lot to do with my father," he said. "There's something I should have told you—something you need to know that concerns my brother's will and is the reason I'm so worried about my father. I should have told you sooner—when we first met—but I didn't know you then. And later it always seemed the wrong time… No, that's not right. The truth is I was afraid you'd think I was just here trying to take advantage of you and Maggie and I didn't want that."

He pulled himself away from her, stretching his legs out in front of him as he looked out over the park.

"I'd never think that. I know you care about Maggie. Just *tell* me. What is it that I need to know?" she asked, knowing that whatever it was it had something to do with his desire for them to marry.

"When Michael died he didn't have much. He'd gone through most of the money we had inherited from our grandparents. But he still had the shares in the family business he inherited when our mother died. When he learned about Maggie he had his will updated, leaving everything to her. Those shares are worth a lot of money, Lana, but more importantly having control of them is worth a lot to my father."

"I don't care about any shares in your father's company, Trent. As far as I'm concerned he can have them. I just want to protect my daughter."

"The will specifies that Maggie is to keep them until she turns twenty-one. Then she can do whatever she wants with them. For now Michael's lawyers are in charge of them—till custody is decided by the courts. And that's where we are right now. The court can decide on only one of us. When my father decides to get involved in the custody battle—and he will, I promise you—we could both lose. This way we can both be there to protect Maggie."

"Of course after the case is settled we can both go back to our old lives, but until then we'd have to play the part of a loving couple for the court's sake."

Of course he would go back to his life in Houston. Had she really thought a man like Trent would be interested in actually setting up a home with her? It was only his sense of responsibility that had him willing to do something as drastic as marrying her.

She knew she shouldn't be hurt that he had come up with what might be the solution to all their problems. She should be happy that he was willing to go this far for his niece. But playing a part for the court? Living together day in and day out? How could she do that without falling for the man completely?

"I need to think about it," she said. "You should have told me everything before, Trent. For me to even consider this we need to be honest with each other."

"I'll do anything I can for you and Maggie," he said. "You know that."

Anything, but love us. How could she go into an agreement like this without her feelings for him getting stronger? But how could she not when this might ensure that Maggie would always be hers?

"I need some time," she said.

As she stood to leave she watched Trent as he walked over to the sandbox to get Maggie. He would be such a good father—a great father—but would that be enough?

She had so much to consider before she could make a decision of this magnitude. She would have to talk to Nathan so that she would know the legal requirements, and she would have to come up with some guidelines for their relationship. She knew she needed to protect her daughter, but if she was to survive this fake marriage she would have to find a way to protect herself too.

She had already let herself get too close to Trent. If she took this step it would just make her more vulnerable. Could she take that chance? Could she survive another heartbreak? She wasn't sure she would.

A scream cut through her thoughts and she turned to see Trent, still holding Maggie, running toward a young woman holding a limp child.

Lana caught up with him and reached for Maggie, freeing his arms to take the child. As he knelt beside him Lana looked up at the woman whose face was filled with horror. She knew her. Sally—or was it Sandy?—and her little boy came to the park often when she was there with Maggie. They'd talked a few times, sharing something cute or horrible that their kids had recently done.

Shoving Maggie into the mom's arms, she leaned down to see if she could help.

"What happened?" Trent asked the mother.

Lana watched him check the child's breathing, then his pulse.

"Call 911," he said.

"He was playing, just running around like normal. Then he coughed…he kind of coughed… I don't know…he sounded funny… And then he fell… I thought he was playing…just playing." The woman sobbed as she clutched Maggie to her.

Lana watched as Trent assessed the child even as she gave their address to the operator on the line. "Pulse?" she asked.

"Too slow," Trent said.

"An ambulance is on its way," she told him, and she continued to hold the phone, giving the operator a play-by-play on the situation.

"Any history of asthma?" he asked the mother.

"No. He just fell down…" the mother said.

Trent was about to give the child a breath, then he paused. Lana watched as he glanced around the sidewalk. Following his gaze, she saw the apple core at the same time he did.

"Was he eating an apple?" she asked the mom.

"An apple?" the mom said.

Lana could tell the mother was going into shock, panic overwhelming her.

"Could he have choked on an apple?" Trent asked as he opened the child's mouth and looked inside. "Nothing," he said to Lana.

"Yes!" the mother said. "I gave him an apple for a snack. Oh, God, is that it?" The mother was now sobbing.

Maggie whimpered in the woman's arms and the woman held her tighter, unconsciously soothing her with her hands.

Trent positioned his hands on the child's body, then thrust up several times before returning to the child's mouth.

"I've got it," he said as he pulled out a piece of apple and threw it on the ground. Then he gave the child a couple of breaths and they both watched as the small chest rose with each one.

The child suddenly started to cough—a sound as sweet as the most beautiful music Lana had ever heard.

Trent checked the little boy's pulse then looked up to Lana and smiled. "His pulse is stronger," he said.

The child opened his eyes and then took in all the people surrounding him and started crying for his mother.

Lana took Maggie from the woman so that she could hold her son, then reached over and hugged Trent to her.

"I'm so glad you were here," she said, and reached over and gave him what had to be the biggest kiss she'd ever given him, ending it with an audible smack.

"Me too," Maggie said, and she planted soft baby kisses on Lana's laughing face and then Trent's, before he moved away to talk to the ambulance team who had arrived.

Lana held Maggie close as other people in the park approached her, asking what had happened, and watched Trent help the crew load the little boy on a stretcher. The mother gave Trent a hug and thanked him.

Trent was a good man. He had saved this

woman's child. He was prepared to marry her so they could protect her little girl. The truth was that a fake marriage was more than she had ever expected. Yet the thought of faking something as important as marriage didn't sit right with her.

If she couldn't have the real thing, could she settle for an imitation?

Trent walked out of the nursery and felt like a jerk even before the door had closed behind him. He had been short with the nurses for days now. Baby Hope had not made the progress he would have liked to see, and that along with the pressure of waiting for his father to make his next move was getting to him.

Of course his bad mood didn't have *anything* to do with the fact that Lana hadn't jumped at the chance to be Mrs. Montgomery. Sure it didn't.

He decided that he would walk up to Labor and Delivery and check on the laboring patients there. And if he just happened to run into Lana up on the unit that would be okay. It was time for her to make a decision…time for both of them to move on to the next step that would secure the future for her and for Maggie.

"Kat told me you were on the unit," Lana said as she walked into the break room.

"How does that woman always know where I am?" Trent asked as he poured himself a cup of coffee. He started to offer Lana a cup, then remembered she preferred tea.

"I wouldn't be surprised if she knew where every good-looking warm male body in this hospital is right now. It's just a talent she has," Lana said.

"You doing okay?" he asked her as she moved from the table to open the fridge and then shut it. She was as nervous as the mares at the ranch when they were about to be mounted by one of the studs.

Suddenly memories of their lovemaking flooded his mind. Okay, he really *didn't* need that in his thoughts right now.

"Lana, come here," he ordered her.

She was a nervous wreck, and he needed to find out what he could do to settle her down. Was this what the thought of marrying him did to her? So much for all his charm and good looks.

Pulling her close to him, he moved his hand down her soft cheek, then tilted her chin up till her troubled green eyes were forced to meet his. The feel of her body against him had his body responding instantly, while at the same time the emotional strain that had plagued him for the past few days eased away.

"Someone could come in," Lana said, and pulled away. "I got a call from Ms. Nelson," she told him.

"And…?" Trent asked as he moved closer.

"He's done it," Lana said.

She looked at him with eyes shadowed with the dark circles that told him he wasn't the only one not sleeping these days.

"Your father's lawyers contacted her today to see where the custody process stood," she said.

"She hasn't contacted me yet," he said as he pulled his phone out of the back pocket of his scrubs and checked to see if he had any missed calls. "Or she called my lawyer and he hasn't had time to pass on the information yet. I don't want to pressure you," he went on, "but if we're going to have any chance of pulling off this marriage for the benefit of the court you're going to have to make a decision soon."

* * *

Marriage to Trent. It was the only thing she had thought of since that day at the park. It wasn't a terrible idea. And she did see the advantages it would give them. With her history with Maggie, and Trent's biological relationship, together and presenting a happy home for her daughter, they would have a good chance against anything his father might throw against them.

But would she be able to pull it off? She wasn't a good actor. Her drama grades in high school would attest to that. But surely they should be able to play the role without much effort? She would have to be comfortable with Trent touching her in public, and with showing the normal affection a couple in love would share, playing the happy newlyweds. It would hurt, but she could do it.

Yet still she couldn't bring herself to say yes.

There would be real problems after the marriage was over and Trent went back to his old life, but that wasn't what was stopping her. The problem was that even after all the warnings she had given herself she was falling in love with Trent a little bit more every time she saw him. How was she going to be able to hide the way she felt from him if they were living together?

Part of her wanted to believe that he cared for her too. She had to believe that he cared for her in some way, or he wouldn't be willing to go to such extreme measures. And there was no doubt that they got along well together in bed. He had never mentioned that it would be a marriage in name only, and just the thought of being back in his bed made her want to agree, but she knew that the intimacy between them would just make it harder to walk away later, when the need for their marriage was over.

She was willing to sacrifice everything for Maggie, but surely there had to be another way.

"I know," she said as she pulled away from him. "I just need a little longer."

Trent threw his jacket across the back of the first chair he came to when he got home. An emergency Caesarean section had come in right when he had been about to get off, and he had volunteered to stay and help out.

He saw the blinking light flashing on his answering machine, but decided to get himself a cold bottle of water from the fridge before he checked to see who had left a message. He had given the number here to only a few people since he was only in town temporarily.

He took a refreshingly clean swallow of water, then picked up the phone to check the message. His stomach twisted itself into tight knots as he listened.

He ran his hands through his hair, then began to undress. His father was coming to town and there was nothing he could do about it. Lana would have to give him an answer—and soon. There was no telling what his father was planning and he would have to be prepared for anything—including telling Lana about what he intended for Maggie's inheritance.

But how did he bring that up with her? *Oh, by the way, I forgot to tell you that I plan to use Maggie's share of my family's oil company to get revenge on her grandfather for ruining her father's life.*

Would Lana really believe that a man she had known only for a few weeks was more concerned about his niece's welfare than an inheritance worth millions? Would *he* if he was in her shoes? Had he really come with Maggie's welfare as his priority he could have returned to Houston as soon as he had gotten to know Lana and seen how much she loved the little girl, but instead he'd let his own personal experiences with his parents cloud his judgment.

One look at Michael's little girl and he had been reminded of how his brother had been treated by their father, so he had continued with his plan to grab custody of Maggie before his father could get involved.

What had he been thinking?

Lana caught sight of Trent as he entered the cafeteria. He smiled at her as he headed over to her table, but she noticed his high-voltage smile had been turned down to just a low-wattage gleam today, and his eyes had the same look she was becoming accustomed to seeing in her own mirror.

Stress was beginning to take its toll on both of them.

"May I sit down?" he asked as he approached.

She wasn't sure what had him doubting his welcome. She was thinking about *marrying* the man, for heaven's sake, and yet now he was back to acting as if they were strangers?

"Sure. Is everything all right?" she asked as

she watched him lay his tray on the plastic table and then arrange his food.

"Yeah—why?" he asked as he looked up at her.

"You just don't seem like yourself today," Lana said, and she reached out and covered one of his hands with her own. "What is it, Trent?"

Trent looked around at the other staff and visitors sitting at the tables and then back at her. Whatever was bothering him clearly wasn't something he wanted to discuss in public. Was it the fake marriage? Or was it something his father had done?

She placed her fork back down on the table, the thought of having to deal with more complications in her fight to keep Maggie dulling her appetite.

She started to remove her hand from where it lay over his, then stopped when he turned his hand over and gave hers a slight squeeze. She'd have to wait till they were alone to find out what had caused this change in him.

"Eat your lunch," Lana said as she removed her hand from his. "Though I'm warning you: the tuna surprise is a step down from the fried potato casserole."

"So I've been told," Trent said as he picked up his own fork and stared down into the pale-looking noodles and sauce.

They ate in silence, with Lana just moving her food around on her plate while she watched him somehow manage to finish the cafeteria's special of the day. As they went to drop off their dirty trays she tried to think of somewhere they could go and not be interrupted.

She needed to know what had happened to cause this change in him. And there was one place where no one in the hospital would see or hear them and they could have the privacy they needed.

It was risky, going down there, but it would be worth it if she could find out what was bothering him. They would talk, she promised herself as the idea formed. *Just talk.*

"You got a few minutes?" Lana asked as they walked side by side down the hall that led to the bank of elevators that went up to the patient care floors.

"I'm checked out on the roster for the rest of this hour," Trent said as he studied his watch. "Why?"

She could tell that he was shocked when she

grabbed his hand and pulled him away from the main elevators and down the hall to where one old, dented metal elevator door stood.

Okay, maybe they'd do a little more than talk. Maybe she would kiss his sad mood away…just a few kisses to bring the warmth back into that spectacular smile of his…and then they'd talk.

They'd had such little time alone together lately, and she couldn't help but feel that he was pulling away from her. And if she decided that she couldn't go through with a fake marriage, where would that leave them? She'd had a taste of Trent and she wanted more. Whether or not she agreed to marry him everything between them would soon change. She needed just one more time alone with him before that happened.

"You want to show me the freight elevator?" Trent asked.

The doors opened and Lana pulled on his hand until he reluctantly got into the elevator. She pushed the button that took the elevator to the basement, and then froze when the reality of what she was doing hit her.

What she was doing was crazy and dangerous, but she wouldn't let that stop her. She'd have to give him an answer soon and then everything between them would change. She needed to be held in his arms one more time. Because she knew in her heart that it would have to be the last time, no matter what she decided about marrying him.

When the doors opened Lana poked her head outside to make sure there wasn't anyone around to see where they were headed. Looking both ways, she was relieved to see that they were alone. She pulled Trent out of the elevator with her.

"Okay, now I'm getting a little freaked out," Trent said as he pointed to the arrow indicating the hospital morgue.

"It's not that way," Lana said, and began walking down the opposite hall.

It had to be close to here. She had heard one of the nurses talking about it not long after she had come to work there, and then one of the labor and delivery nurses had dragged her along on a dare —to see if the room really existed or if it was just an urban legend.

"If you tell me what you're looking for maybe I can help you."

"It's right here," Lana said as she made one

more turn and then saw the door she was looking for.

"What *is* this?" he asked.

Lana tried the doorknob and was relieved when it turned easily. She had gotten her nerve up and she didn't want to lose it now. She pulled Trent in by the hand she was still holding, then shut the door quickly before she flipped the light switch and locked the door behind them.

"It's the hospital make-out room," she said, and smiled when she saw the shock hit his face.

Trent glanced around at the mix of broken furniture filling the room. Looking back at sweet, honest-to-the-core little Lana, he watched as she seemed to turn into a siren right before his eyes.

"We need to *talk*, Lana," Trent said as he pulled away.

"You see this door?" she said as she leaned back against it.

Surely she couldn't mean what she was about to say? With everything that was going on with them right now?

Guilt slammed through him as warning bells began to toll inside his overstimulated body.

This wasn't right. He had planned to tell her everything—come clean about his plan to use Michael's will against his father, and tell her everything that he should have told her long before they had gotten to this point. He wanted everything out in the open so that there was nothing hidden between the two of them and the decision she had to make.

"We leave everything and everybody on the other side of this door," she continued. "Can you do that?"

"Lana, we need to talk." Trent said again.

He was going to tell her all the reasons this wasn't a good idea. He would swear in a court of law that he was. But then she walked over to him and laid one small finger against his lips.

"We'll talk later," Lana said. "I promise."

Trent tried once more to stop things from going any farther, and then she stood on her tiptoes and whispered in his ear.

"I *need* you, Trent. Do you need me?"

Urgent desire struck him as her warm, sweet breath blew into his ear. If he'd been a better man then maybe, just maybe, he could have withstood the want that flashed through him as her lips worked their way down the side of his neck.

But he had a weakness where Lana was concerned. One moment alone with that sweet body of hers and he was done for. Somehow he had let his desire for her seep deep down inside him—until he could no longer control the need that flared up and consumed him.

"Yes," he answered as he lifted her up so that he could meet her lips.

The taste of her filled him as his tongue circled with hers. He had missed this—her—so much. He tilted his head to let his tongue delve deeper into her mouth, then crushed her body to his and took the weight of it.

The feel of her returning his kisses with the same feverish need that he felt had him losing control too fast, so he pulled back. Her moan of protest was almost too much for him, and for a moment he thought of just taking her right there, against the wall.

Barely managing to clamp down on his body's demand that he take her *now*, he pulled away from her. Looking around the small room, he saw a dilapidated plastic chair within reach. He used one of his feet to hook one of the chair legs and pull it close.

As he sat down with Lana in his arms he arranged her body so that she faced him, with her legs straddling his body. When her hand reached down between them and pulled the cord that held his scrub pants closed he lifted her and hiked up her skirt. He let his hand run down the thin line of her thong then pushed it aside so that his fingers could slide deep inside her.

A hot bolt of desire ran the length of him as her hand circled him and his groan filled the room. He ran his hand once more between her legs, then pushed her hand aside as he lifted her until he could feel his tip at her entrance. Thrusting up, he brought her down on the full, hard length of him in one swift move.

He stopped and took a moment to look at the flushed face and bruised lips of this woman who had clearly caused him to lose his mind.

And then she started to move.

This was so much more then she had planned but, oh, it felt so good to be with him like this again.

Lana eased herself down around him as she stared into his eyes. Never had she felt such an intimate connection as she did at this moment. In this stark room, totally absent of any romance, it was as if they were the only two people in the world.

She let him increase speed as he tightened his hands against her hips, and her breath caught with each stroke as she fought to keep her suddenly heavy eyes open. She loved the feel of him sliding in and out of her, loved the sweet, almost painful stretch of her body deep down inside her.

She could feel her body tightening around him, but she fought against it. She forced her eyes to stay open, letting herself drown in his deep blue eyes as his body stroked her into unbearable pleasure. His hands came up and cupped her breasts, then he bent his head and took her lips with such hunger that it destroyed her.

It was too much for her to take—too much for her to withstand. Her hands gripped his hair and she tried to pull his mouth closer. The demand of his lips, the hard length of him as he drove deep inside her, filled her completely.

Her breath caught, then held. This was too much. He was taking her too far.

She felt herself losing her hold as she soared higher and higher, her core tightening, her body reaching for its climax. She tightened her arms around him, holding on to him as if her life was dependent on that connection between them, the joining of their bodies anchoring her to him. He thrust into her once more and her body shattered into a million pieces.

CHAPTER TEN

LANA, WHO HAD NEVER had the privilege of experiencing the walk of shame before, snuck into the back entrance of her unit. Trent had reassured her that she looked great, but she knew there was no way she could look the same coming out as she had going into that storage room.

Had she lost her mind? Thank goodness none of the other midwives she worked with, were in the office. They would have seen right through her casual act. All she would have had to do was look one of them in the eye and she knew she'd spill everything.

It wasn't every day that she managed to have mind-blowing sex in the most scandalous of places. Was it just a few weeks ago that she had been calling her life boring?

She knew that making love with Trent again had added more complications, but she would never regret it. She didn't even want to *think* about what the consequences of their getting caught together would have been. But at the same time it seemed she had spent too much of her time worrying about what the staff were saying about her and Trent. Why not give them something to really talk about?

Not that she would actually *tell* anyone about what had happened between the two of them, but she might as well be guilty of some of the rumors going around about them.

But what had been wrong with him today before the mind-blowing sex? He had become known around the hospital for having a big smile and a quick sense of humor. Even in the fight they'd had in the court he had still been friendly to her.

Not that she had always been the same with him. And she wouldn't apologize for that. She'd had every right to be angry with him when he had first come to town. But she hadn't been able to stay mad at him for long. Watching the gentle man he was while caring for the smallest of babies, and the way he eased the concern of anxious mothers, and then seeing him interact with Maggie, it had just become too hard for her to hold a grudge against him.

He had looked much more relaxed when

they'd parted—or at least until he had stopped her before she got on the elevator and reminded her that she couldn't avoid making a decision about their marriage much longer.

She'd seen the stress return then. Had he sensed the conflict inside her?

The consequences of *not* going through with the marriage were so high that she knew she shouldn't even be considering turning him down. She should agree to Trent's plan and just hope she would be able to find the strength to survive when everything was over between them.

But how would that be possible when her heart already hurt at the thought of him leaving?

If she'd felt that Trent had even the slightest desire to marry her for any other reason than to protect his niece, she would jump at the chance. But that wasn't the case, and she needed to get over any daydreams she was having of them being together as a family and accept the inevitable.

Trent was only interested in marriage because of his need to protect his niece—which was as honorable a sacrifice as anyone could make.

But she had vowed after her break-up with Joe that she would never let someone make her feel that marrying her would be a sacrifice. She had always wanted to have someone love her just the way she was, but maybe it was time to accept that wasn't ever going to happen.

She grabbed the lab coat she kept hanging on the back of her office door and put it on to help hide the wrinkles that she had in her skirt and then headed down to the reception area to call for her first afternoon appointment. Everything in her personal life was coming to a head, but life kept going. Women continued to get pregnant, and that meant there were still babies who needed her to be there to deliver them.

As Trent rounded the corner of the Labor and Delivery nurses' station he saw Lana as she was coming out of one of the labor rooms, and he watched her as she spoke with the family members who had been waiting outside the patient's door. She was wearing scrubs today, so he knew she was planning on spending most of her time on the unit.

"Hey, Trent," one of the nurses called as they walked up beside him. "We're almost ready to go back if you want to meet us in the operating room."

"I'll be right there," he said, and turned to walk toward Lana.

She gave him a little wave, then walked back into the labor room. He'd have to catch her after they'd finished the next delivery.

The surgery went off without any problems, and in less than an hour another mother was holding a perfect little baby in her arms as her husband took pictures to show the rest of the family in the waiting room. He checked at the nurses' station and found that Lana had just gone into another delivery.

"You have a great team here," Trent told Dr. Miller as he joined him at the nurses' station to finish his paperwork.

"They're a great group of nurses," Dr. Miller said as he looked up from the chart he was checking for his notes. "I've heard you're here just for one a short time," the doctor said as he stretched back in his chair. "You ought to consider staying."

"I'm here for an eight-week assignment right now," Trent said. "I have a permanent position in Houston."

He turned as Lana came into the nurses' station. She walked over to some of the nurses who were talking.

"We'd be happy to have you stay," Dr. Miller said. "Good pediatricians are hard to find."

The doctor rose out of his chair, then turned to see where Trent's attention had gone.

"Just think about it," he said. Smiling, the man gave Trent a hearty slap on the back and left the unit.

Trent was glad to see Lana heading over to where he stood leaning against the station's countertop. He nodded his head toward the exit door and then accompanied her out of the unit. He only had a few minutes before he needed to get back and take the next case in the operating room.

"Lana, I—"

"Look, I've got to get back to the office right now, but why don't you come over tonight? You can see Maggie and I'll fix dinner."

They came to the elevator doors just as one opened its doors with the button's light showing it was headed up. A group of visitors bearing flowers and pastel-pink-wrapped presents walked out, pushing the two of them together.

Her body brushed against his, sending a quick burst of desire through him.

Desire he couldn't act on. Not here, not now.

He reached out to tuck a loose piece of hair behind her ear and let his hand linger on the soft lobe, then slide down the side of her neck.

"Trent…?"

The hoarse whisper of his name was too much. Before he could do something that would surely shock the staff he pulled away from her.

"Tonight," he said.

Turning away, he headed for the stairs. Maybe a little physical activity would get him cooled down before he made it to the OR.

Lana was in a better mood when she got home. She'd made peace with her decision concerning Trent's marriage proposal and, while she was nervous, she knew she was doing the right thing.

She'd taken Maggie with her to the grocery store, where she'd bought all the ingredients for one of her daughter's favorite pasta dishes.

"Hey, you're home!" Lana said as Amanda walked out of the house.

"Class was canceled tonight," Amanda said

as she reached over and took the toddler out of Lana's arms.

"Thanks. I bought a few more groceries then I had planned." Lana juggled the bags in her arms, then reached back into the car for the last two.

"Yeah, it looks like you're going to feed an army," Amanda said. "Did Momma invite a football team over for supper?"

Maggie laughed up at her babysitter, then struggled to get down as soon as they made it inside the house. The toddler ran down the hall to her room as soon as she was let down, then was back in seconds, pushing her plastic play shopping cart around the kitchen, where the bags of food had been taken.

"No, but I did invite Trent," Lana said.

"Are you sure that's a good idea?" Amanda asked.

"Have you gotten a *look* at the man?" she teased her friend, and then stopped as she saw the look of confusion on her face.

"Okay, I know this is hard to understand," Lana said as she walked around the room, putting everything in its proper place.

"It just seems like you're getting more and more involved with him," said Amanda.

"Does it?" Lana asked.

She began sorting through the vegetables she would need to get ready for the evening's meal.

"Lana, are you okay?" Amanda had walked over to the sink and was staring at her as if she had grown a second head. "Oh, my God—you're in love with the guy."

"I didn't say that," Lana insisted.

She began slicing a tomato on the wooden butcher block, making sure that she had a good excuse not to look up at her friend.

"You didn't have to. I can see it," Amanda said.

Lana felt the heat of the blush that she knew stained her cheeks.

"Have you had sex with him?"

Looking up, she watched Amanda's eyes go wide before a big grin spread across her face.

"I can't *believe* it. You've had sex with the hunky Dr. Montgomery!"

"Hey, no S-word in front of Maggie," Lana said, hoping to change the subject—as if that was going to happen now.

"So the rumors about you two hooking up

were true?" Amanda asked as she went over to the table to sit down. "I want details."

"I'm not telling you about—" Lana stopped as Amanda doubled over with laughter. Crap—the brat had tricked her. She knew there was no way she would share what was going on between her and Trent.

She didn't even know for sure herself what it was that was happening between them. It was as if they had two separate relationships. In one they were talking about marriage as if it were a business arrangement between the two of them. In the other they weren't only friendly…they couldn't keep their hands off each other.

No—they both had to leave their personal issues out this. Maggie had to be their priority.

Lana ignored her friend's teasing for the rest of the day. Amanda was just having a good time, picking on her, but deep down Lana knew her friend was right. Even after all the warnings she had given herself, she had fallen head over heels in love with a cowboy doctor who had come to town to break her heart.

CHAPTER ELEVEN

LANA WAS SURPRISED at how smoothly the meal had gone. If only their next conversation would go as smoothly.

Dinnertime with a tired toddler could quickly turn into a messy, crying affair, but instead of running from the house screaming Trent had pitched in and helped.

Deciding to give him a realistic view of parenting, she had assigned him the task of bathing Maggie while she cleaned up the kitchen. He'd survived his one day alone with the toddler, but that was different from the day-in and day-out demands of parenting. The sight of him drenched to the waist and grinning madly as he held a sparkling clean Maggie had sent her into uncontrollable fits of laughter.

"She's really asleep this time," he said now, as he joined her back in the kitchen.

"You sure she's not playing possum again?" she asked.

"Hey, I happen to be an expert on child behavior," he said.

She looked up from the sink and raised an eyebrow.

"Okay, she fooled me once," he said, "but I'm on to her tricks now. She's definitely destined for the big screen when she grows up."

"I'm thinking more of her as a teenage drama queen," she said.

One look at his horrified face had her laughing again. "You do realize she's going to grow up some day?" she said.

"I don't want to even *think* about it," he said.

She didn't either. It seemed like only days ago that Maggie had learned to crawl. Now she was walking everywhere, and learning a new word daily. Next there would be school, then boys… *Boys?* She definitely wasn't ready to think about *that*.

"You were great with her tonight—well, except for the half-hour it took you to actually get her into her crib," she said, "But that's not really your fault. She knew you'd be an easy mark so she played you."

"But those were *real* tears," he protested.

"That she quickly turned off as soon as I

walked into the room. Like I said—she played you."

Trent took the glass of tea Lana offered and sat at the small table, waiting for Lana to sit down too. Finally they would have a chance to discuss their plans to keep his father out of Maggie's life.

He knew Lana had reservations about the idea of marrying him, but he knew they would be able to make things work out together. They were both level-headed adults. There would be none of the dysfunction of his parents' marriage.

Still, it would be for the best if they ironed out some of the details. If they set up the terms of their marriage now it would be easier for both of them, but for some reason the more they tried to make this feel like a business deal the more uncomfortable he felt.

He put his hands in his pocket and felt for the ring he meant to surprise her with. He tightened his hand around it, then let go and pulled his hand out.

This was what he wanted. No drama, no chaos, no fights that ended with one of them crying or, worse, one of them dead. They needed to keep this separate from any feelings they might have for each other. They were putting a good plan in motion and sticking to it so there would be no misunderstandings.

"So, have you come to a decision?" he asked. He felt his pulse quicken as he waited for her to answer.

From the hesitancy before Lana's response he knew she was uncertain, but that was to be expected. Most people didn't go into marriage like the two of them were doing. Of course most people weren't in the situation they were in either.

Trent watched her as she seemed to gather herself together. This wasn't going to be easy for either of them, but it would be harder if they didn't start off on the right foot.

"Trent," she said, "I want you to know how much I appreciate your offer. I know you'd do anything for Maggie."

Trent watched her as she took a sip of tea, a sinking feeling invading his chest.

"That's why I think we can work things out between us so that we don't have to do anything as drastic as getting married," she went on.

"I don't understand. If we married everything would be taken care of," he said.

"Stop and think about it, Trent. What about after the adoption? After you go back to Houston? We'd be right back at the same place we are now, trying to work out custody of Maggie. We can't do that again. It's not fair to either of us and it certainly isn't fair to Maggie."

"I promise this is not some type of trick. I'm not trying to take Maggie away from you, Lana. You're her mother. The only one she will ever know. I lived most of my childhood without a mother—I don't want that for Maggie. But I still want to be part of her life. This way I can be."

"And what are we going to tell Maggie when suddenly you're not there every day? How will that make her feel, Trent? She'll just be more confused. It's not right to do that to her. But if we work together and show the court that you support my adopting her we can both do what's right for her. Maggie can live with me and still have an awesome uncle who she goes to visit and who spoils her as any uncle would. Instead of being confused about your part in her life, she'll have the security of being loved by the two of us. And with you handling her inheritance I know she'll be taken care of just as your brother wanted."

He got up from the table, unable to sit still any longer. He didn't want to confuse Maggie—he just wanted to protect her. And Lana. Why couldn't she see that this was the answer to keeping Maggie safe from his father?

"We wouldn't have to end the marriage immediately," he said as he began to pace.

"Listen to yourself," Lana said as she stood up and joined him. "You're already changing things. Can't you see how complicated marriage would make things between us?"

"It wouldn't have to be that way. We can set out the terms of the marriage. Have a lawyer draw it up, if you like, to make it all legal if you don't trust me."

He heard the bitterness in his voice, but couldn't control it.

"It's not that I don't trust you—it's that I don't trust myself," she said as she shook her head.

"What does *that* mean?" he asked, even more confused now. If she truly trusted him why wouldn't she marry him?

* * *

Lana had expected Trent to try and get her to change her mind, to see the reasons he thought this was the best thing to do for Maggie, but she had never thought he would be this upset.

The man standing in front of her was not the Trent she knew, who always remained calm and controlled no matter what was going on around him. This man was anything but calm, with his body coiled tight, his face a beautiful mix of confusion and frustration, his hands running through his thick dark hair.

Hair she'd once run her hands through. Hair she'd never have the right to touch again after tonight.

Her body heated with memories of tangling her hands in Trent's hair as she pulled him closer, as she anchored her lips to his, felt his tongue deep inside her mouth, his hands roaming her body. Those were the other times she'd glimpsed this man in front of her now.

She watched as he took a deep breath, then walked over to her and took her hands in his. How could she continue this relationship without him utterly destroying her heart? How could she make him see that faking a marriage with him was impossible for her without telling him what she felt for him?

"What *is* it? What do you mean you don't trust yourself?" he asked, his voice now calm and caring. "I would trust you with anything."

"Anything?" she asked, her heart stuttering as she took the biggest risk she'd ever taken. "Would you trust me with your heart?"

"What?" he asked as he pulled his hands from hers.

"I don't want to settle for a fake marriage, Trent. I want a real marriage. A marriage like my parents', where you plan to grow old together, a marriage filled with love and respect."

"And what would *I* know about those types of marriages, Lana?"

She could hear the bitterness in his voice. She couldn't blame him for being bitter. He'd been given a raw deal as a child. But he wasn't a child any longer. He needed to see that things could be different for him.

"I know your parents' marriage wasn't perfect..."

"That's an understatement. It was a war zone, with me and my brother as prisoners. I'll never live like that again."

"But that's not what marriage has to be. When two people love each other they can make it work. Yeah, they might argue and disagree sometimes, but they also learn how to compromise and support each other. That's what I want, Trent. Not a marriage filled with lies. I want someone to be there when things are good, but also to be by my side when things go wrong. I want someone to love me no matter what. In sickness and in health."

"Till death do us part?" Trent asked, and the sarcasm in his voice was almost palpable.

"Yes, that," she said.

"And you think you could have that with *me*?" Trent asked, his eyes wide as he backed further away from her. "This was supposed to be about Maggie—not about us."

"And it was—until I fell in love with you," she said, her hands covering her heart, as if to protect it from the pain she knew would come.

It hurt to see the panic in his eyes, but she'd known before she'd admitted her feelings for him that he wasn't ready for this—not for any type of real commitment, let alone one that included messy emotions such as love.

How long had it been since someone had told

him that they loved him? Months? Years? Had anyone really, truly, *ever* loved this man the way he deserved? She knew he could love—she'd seen it in his eyes every time he looked at Maggie—but did he know how to *accept* love?

"I love you, Trent," she said, and her voice was stronger as she poured everything she felt for him into it. "I love the way you comfort your patients' parents when they're scared and worried, the way your eyes light up with laughter when you're playing with Maggie, and the way you want to protect her so much that you're willing to marry me—even if it is for all the wrong reasons. I love the way you make me laugh, the way you have of calming my worries, the way you make me feel like a whole woman when I'm in your arms."

"It's not you…" he said.

"I know it's not. It's about you being afraid to take a chance on us. Life's all about chances, Trent. Do you know how hard it is for me to stand here and wait for you to reject me like Joe did?"

"Joe was stupid," he mumbled.

"Yes, he was—but I didn't see that until I met you. You made me see that I could have it all if I was willing to take a chance. I just need to know if you can take that same chance with me."

She waited as Trent looked at her, sadness in his eyes.

"I don't think I can give you what you need," he said.

She watched him reached his hand into his pocket, then slide it back out again, empty.

"I don't know how to be what you want… what you deserve."

"Yes, you do," she whispered as he walked away from her. "You just don't know it."

Lana tried to keep her mind on the patient's chart that she was updating. She'd been having a hard time concentrating since the night Trent had walked out of her house. It had been two days now and she hadn't heard from him.

She'd spent hours second-guessing her decision to refuse Trent. Would it have been so bad to take what he had offered? To have what time with him she could have, even though she knew it would have ended with a broken heart?

A knock at her office door sent her thoughts back to the present, where they needed to be.

"Come in," she called as a second knock sounded.

"Hey, Lana, there's a Mr. Montgomery is here to see you," the young receptionist said as she stepped into the room.

"Send him in, Lily." Lana stood and removed her lab coat, then straightened her skirt, her hands unsteady. Trent had never been to her office before and she couldn't imagine why he was there now. Could he have realized that she was right?

The man who walked into her office wasn't Trent, but she had no doubt that he was a Montgomery. His face was so like his son's, in all its lines and angles, but it was aged and hardened. His brown eyes were cold, so unlike the warm blue of Trent's, and the straight line of his lips showed no hint of humor.

He wore an expensive suit that screamed power, and his large six-foot frame overwhelmed her small office. Now she understood why Trent had been so worried about his father's interest in Maggie. If this man wanted something, he'd take it. But he wouldn't be taking her daughter anywhere.

"Mr. Montgomery—come in." Surprised

when her voice came out with no trace of a tremor, she indicated the chair in front of her desk with a wave of her shaky hand.

"Please have a seat," she said, then waited till he sat before sitting down in her own chair.

"Thank you," he said as he folded his body into the small chair.

She watched as he looked around the room, taking in the setting as if preparing for battle. His eyes stopped on the bulletin board behind her, where she displayed pictures of the babies that she had delivered. She knew the second his eyes found the picture she had added just that morning.

It had been taken on one of their trips to the park and it showed Maggie giggling with joy on one of the toddler swings. But it had been the look on Trent's face that had caused her to pull her phone out of her purse and snap the picture. He looked so relaxed and free. And *happy*—as if spending the day pushing a swing in the park was just what he wanted to be doing.

"What can I do for you, Mr. Montgomery?" she asked.

"I'm sure you know I'm here about my granddaughter," he said.

"Maggie's fine. She's a beautiful, healthy little girl," she said. "If you'd like to meet her I'm sure me and Trent can arrange it."

"I was under the impression that you had sole custody of the child at this time."

"I do, but Trent has become a very important part of our lives," she said. "We discuss everything concerning Maggie together."

His cold eyes melted with the heat of the temper that flared there now. *Why?* Why couldn't the man just be happy that his granddaughter was going to be taken care of?

Being studied like a bug under a microscope was uncomfortable and she was tired of it. "Mr. Montgomery, if you didn't come here to arrange to see Maggie then why *did* you come?"

The smile on his lips didn't touch his eyes. How could a man so cold and calculating have raised a son like Trent? Of course the obvious answer to that was that he hadn't raise him.

"I came to make you an offer."

An offer?" she said. What was he going to do? Offer to *buy* her daughter?

"My youngest son…"

"Michael… Maggie's father," she said, with a hint of annoyance evident in her voice.

"I do know my son's name, Ms. Sanders. No matter what *Trent* has told you…" he emphasized the name "…I do care for my sons. Both of them."

"I'm sorry," she said. "And I'm sorry for your loss."

He accepted her apology with a nod of his head.

"As I was saying, Michael made certain stipulations in his will concerning his daughter—Maggie."

His lips parted in a small smile at this acknowledgement of the little girl's name.

"My son apparently wanted to make sure his child was taken care of financially on a long-term basis. Simply put, he left her all his shares in my oil business—shares that could be used to gain control of the company. I'm willing to make an arrangement that would allow you to keep Maggie and still have the financial stability her father wanted for her. I just want the *control* of the shares—not the ownership."

Disbelief filled her. No, this man didn't want to *buy* his granddaughter—instead he was willing to sell her for the right to control some of the shares in his company. No wonder Trent was scared to trust anyone with a father like this man.

"I'm sorry." She stood up abruptly, surprising both of them. She grabbed the top of the, desk using it to steady her. "I'm going to have to ask you to leave. If you want to discuss Maggie's inheritance you'll need to talk to Trent."

He stood and reached into his pocket, then pulled a card from a case and laid it on her desk.

"Here's my contact information. Hopefully we will be able to come to an agreement. I'm sure neither one of us would like to have to take this to court."

CHAPTER TWELVE

TRENT PULLED THROUGH the gated entrance. He was tired and he needed to grab a shower. He'd barely slept since he'd left Lana's house two days ago, and his mind was swirling with thoughts of life without her and Maggie. The only thing that had gone right that day had been with baby Hope's progress. The baby girl was showing herself to be a fighter and if she kept up the progress she had shown in the last couple of days he had no doubt he'd be able to take her off the ventilator by the end of the week. He couldn't help but be inspired by the fight in one so small. He laughed to himself. Baby Hope gave him hope.

The long black car sitting in his driveway had him taking his foot off the gas pedal. There was only one person who would be waiting for him in that limo. His father was in town. That was *just* what he needed to have to deal with today.

He left the front door open for his father to

follow him. It was rude, but it was the mood he was in. Why couldn't his father have called and at least informed him of his visit? Instead now he'd have to deal with everything between the two of them when he was already as tightly wound as a rattlesnake about to strike.

"And hello to you too," his father said as he followed him into the living room.

Trent turned around to face him. He tried to corral the anger that sprang up within him, but it was too strong. He'd held it under such tight control for so long that he was afraid of its power. But he couldn't afford to let his anger at his father take him back to that black hole he had been in when he'd left Texas—before he had met Lana.

Lana and Maggie. They were what was important now.

"Father, I wasn't expecting you." With his thoughts on Lana and little Maggie he felt the anger subside to a manageable irritation.

"Weren't you?" his father asked.

His father took a seat on the sole chair in the room, leaving him to the couch. It was a move he had seen him carry out before. His father was holding court and he was just another one of his subjects, expected to bow down to him.

Trent remained standing.

"I knew you'd be coming eventually, but I expected to hear from your team of lawyers first."

"I find out I have a granddaughter and you expect me to send my *lawyers*? This is something of a personal nature, wouldn't you say?"

Things of a personal nature? Was that what his father was calling family matters now?

"If you'd like to meet Maggie I can see that it is arranged," Trent said.

"The child's foster mother has offered to let me see her and, yes, I would like to meet her. But first I'd like to know what your intentions are concerning the girl and the shares she is to inherit."

"So you've met Lana?"

"Yes, she seems a lovely young woman who has no idea of the worth of my grandchild's inheritance."

"Lana doesn't care about Maggie's portfolio. She loves Maggie for herself."

Just like she loved *him* for himself, he thought.

He bit down on his anger as it returned. "She's one of the most caring women I've ever met and we both owe her our thanks for the way she has taken care of Maggie. She's a genuinely good person. And, unlike most of the people you're used to dealing with, she's honest and sincere."

He could go on and on about what a good person Lana was, but his father would never understand. In his father's world Lana would be considered weak and easy prey. But in the new life Trent had found Lana was all the good things he'd never had in his life. She and Maggie had shown him a whole new world that he could have if he was willing to take a chance.

"And what are your feelings for this woman?" his father asked. "Apart from gratitude."

"I…" He stopped with the word *love* sitting on his tongue. *Love…* Not a word he was comfortable with, or one that he really understood, but it had come to him so easily, so naturally. Was it possible that these crazy feelings he had for Lana were more than just friendship? More than just desire? *Could* it be love? *Was* he in love with her? How would he even know?

But he did. Somehow he knew—had known for a while, if he was honest with himself, that what he felt for her was more than he had felt for anyone else in his life.

"No, Father, it's not gratitude, and it has nothing to do with Maggie or with Michael's will."

He heard his voice rise as he felt joy such as he had never known fill him. *Hell, yeah, it was love.* How had he not known it? If just thinking about her made him feel this good, how could it *not* be? He *loved* Lana Sanders. Not only did he love her, but he was going to marry her if she'd have him. They were going to be a family—him and Lana and Maggie. *His* family.

He looked at the man sitting in the chair inn front of him. He had never understood his father—probably never would—but he couldn't help but feel sorry for him. With all his wealth and power, he was living his life all alone.

They'd both isolated themselves emotionally from others, never letting anyone get close. But then Lana had come into his life and now he was a different man. His life was nothing like his father's and it never would be again.

He needed to tell her. Let her know what she meant to him, how she'd saved him. That he was willing to take a chance on marriage even though it still scared him.

"Look, I don't have time to explain it right now. If the only thing you came for was to see what my intentions are as far as Maggie's shares in the company are concerned, you can relax. I no longer have any plan to use her shares to make a move against you. As long as you agree to let me and Lana adopt her, Maggie's shares will be under the control of the lawyers I'll be setting up for her trust fund. Neither one of us will be able to use them. I won't use your granddaughter against you unless you decide to fight us for custody."

He watched his father's shoulders relax and for the first time noticed how tired his father looked. The man was working himself into an early grave. And for what? More money? More power? Would this have been him thirty years down the road if he hadn't found Lana?

"And now that's settled, I really need to get a shower," said Trent.

He headed off down the hall, then turned around and caught up with his father, who was heading out the door. As his father turned toward him he felt a surge of guilt. He'd dug up a lot of memories lately, and he had to admit that not all of them had been bad. There had been a time before their family had been torn apart when his father had been close to both him and Michael. There was no going back to those times, but he owed it to his brother to give Maggie a chance at a relationship with her grandfather.

"Let me know when you want to meet Maggie. She's a special little girl. I think you'll like her."

"I'm sure I will," his father responded, then started back out the door.

"She has Momma's eyes," Trent said.

His father stopped, then turned back. The glimmer of dampness that filled his father's eyes told him what he needed to know. His father had loved his mother.

He watched his father get into the car, its door being held open by a uniformed driver. No, there was no going back. But maybe with the help of a little girl they could go forward on a different path than the one they had been following all these years.

Lana had folded the same washcloth three times, but she just hadn't got the energy to stop her toddler from playing in the clean laundry.

The visit from Calvin Montgomery had sent her into autopilot. She couldn't even remember the trip home. And, while she'd tried to act normal while she fed and bathed Maggie, she just couldn't keep up the act.

She finally put the child to bed after a quick game of peekaboo with one of the clean towels.

Her whole conversation with the senior Montgomery had been surreal, the man's attention blinded by his greed. How could anyone be so calculating as to offer their granddaughter to a stranger for strictly financial reasons? And how dared he threaten to cause trouble for her with the courts?

She had no intention of letting him intimidate her. She just hoped that she could still depend on Trent to back her up after she'd scared him with her confession of love for him.

A knock on the door startled her out of her dark thoughts.

Opening it, she found a different Trent from the one who had left her house two nights ago. His eyes were bright, his body full of nervous energy, and his smile was dangerous and sexy.

"Can I come in?" he asked as he stood there, one hand in his pocket.

"Of course," she said, and she stepped back from the door, turning her back toward him, unable to meet his eyes.

Having a man run from your house after a declaration of love had a tendency to make things a little awkward.

"Lana, I heard that my father came to see you. I'm sorry if he upset you."

"Upset me?" she said as she walked over to the couch and sat down. "The man was ready to bulldoze me, and when he couldn't do that he threatened to make trouble with my adoption case. I take it he came to see you?"

Trent took a seat on the other end of the couch. She noticed he didn't try to move closer. She'd known there would be no going back after she bared her heart to him. Their relationship was bound to change.

"You won't have to worry about my father anymore. We discussed his concerns and I settled things in a way that he understood. He won't get involved with our adoption of Maggie."

"*Our* adoption?" she asked. Did he still think

she was going to go through with his fake marriage plan? "I thought you understood that I can't marry you, Trent?"

If she sent him away now he'd be lost forever.

"Lana, I will do whatever it takes to protect you and Maggie—that will always be a priority in my life. But I know I messed up, asking you to fake a marriage to me. You were right. A marriage built on lies wouldn't have been fair to either of us. I know that now. And that's not what I want."

Trent rose from the couch and looked down at Lana. What a lucky man he was to have a woman like her love him. He didn't know how to talk about his feelings. It was something they'd have to work on together. But for now hopefully the three little words that had scared him into running away from her just two days ago would be enough.

He knelt down in front of her and pulled the ring he'd been carrying with him for days from his pocket. "Lana, I love you. I want to marry you. And it has nothing to do with my father, the will, or even the adoption. I want to marry you simply because I'm in love you."

"Will you marry me, Lana? Marry me for real?"

Trent had reached out and taken her hand. He *loved* her? He was the prince she had always dreamed of and he *loved* her. The life she had always wanted was just within her reach. But she had to know for sure that he understood what he would be getting.

"We'll never be able to have biological children of our own," she said, feeling her wounded heart stutter as he raised her hand to his lips, then placed it over his heart.

"I'm sorry you had to go through so much when you were young, but I'm thankful that the treatments saved you," he said. "You and Maggie are more family than I ever thought I would have. More than I deserve. The two of you are all I need."

"Are you sure? What if you decide you want to have more children later?"

"We can always adopt—just like we're doing with Maggie," he said. "Lana, we can't build our family on a past that neither of us can change, but we can build it on our future together…on our love for each other."

Could life really be that simple?

"I love you, Trent," she said as she wiped tears from her eyes. "And there's nothing more I want than to marry you."

She watched as he took her hand in his and slid a sparkling ring on her finger. Standing up, he reached down and scooped her up in his arms, silencing her surprised scream with his mouth as he carried her down the hall.

She'd gotten her fairy tale prince and her cowboy all roped together in this man she would soon call her husband. And whether they rode off into the sunset or she was carried away in her prince's arms, she knew they would find their happily-ever-after together.

EPILOGUE

LANA RUSHED UP the courthouse steps. She was going to be late again.

"Don't even say it," she said to Amanda, who was standing at the front door waiting for her.

"Say what? That I told you running off to a delivery wasn't a good idea?" Amanda said.

"You know I had no choice. I've been there for every one of Lacey's deliveries. The fact that this one was going to be a Caesarean section was freaking her out," Lana said as she rushed down the hall toward the courtroom.

Stopping outside the door, she straightened the hemline of the tea dress, then checked her hair in the mirror that Amanda had pulled out of her pocket. The nurses on the unit had all helped her get dressed. Even Kat had helped with her hair and make-up.

"You look beautiful," Amanda said.

Lana smiled at the woman looking back at her from the mirror. It wasn't the perfectly applied make-up, or the hair combed into a flawless knot. No, what she saw was the beauty that only real happiness could bring.

"Ready?" Amanda asked.

"Definitely," Lana said as she opened the heavy wooden door—and stopped.

He wore the same dark suit he'd worn that first day they'd met, with a thin string of a tie he called a *bolo*, and she knew that if she looked down at his feet she'd see a pair of black pointed cowboy boots. In his arms he held a beautiful little girl, dressed in soft pink ruffles.

The sight of the two of them together filled her heart with love. He turned as she entered and the force of his smile almost knocked her over. It was more than she could take. This was her life. How had she got so lucky?

As she walked toward the front of the room she saw her parents, and Trent's great-aunt and uncle, along with Ms. Nelson sitting to one side. They'd decided to make it a quiet ceremony, with a larger reception at the beach to follow.

"Well, here she is," said Judge Hamilton as she approached the bench.

"I'm sorry I'm late, Your Honor," she said.

"Well, I could hold you in contempt of court, I guess, but I think that would make this young man of yours very unhappy."

"Your Honor," Trent said as he shifted Maggie in his arms and took her hand. "I'd be beholden to you if you could show some leniency in this case."

"I promise it won't happen again," said Lana.

"In that case, let's get started," said the stately judge.

"Yes," Lana said as she looked up at Trent and her daughter, "let's get started."

They repeated their vows with hands joined and Maggie at their side, and her sweet giggles filled the courtroom as they shared their first kiss as husband and wife.

Then the judge called the court to order again.

"There's one more piece of business we need to handle," the judge said, "and that's the finalization of this little girl's adoption. Miss Maggie," he said, as Trent lifted her up in his arms so that she could see the judge up close, "do you take your mommy, Lana Montgomery, to be your forever mommy?"

Lana thought her heart would burst from

her chest as she watched her little girl's curls bounce around her head as she nodded yes to the judge.

"And, Miss Maggie, do you take your uncle, Trent Montgomery, to be your forever daddy?"

Astonishment filled the little girl's face, then her mouth lit with a smile and she grabbed Trent's face between her hands. "Daddy!" she squealed, patting his face, and the whole courtroom broke out in laughter.

"You have to answer the judge," her new daddy reminded her.

Turning her head back to the judge, she nodded while Trent reached over and wrapped Lana in his other arm.

"Well, then, by the power invested in me by the State of Florida, I now pronounce you husband and wife, father and mother and daughter, and the cutest darn family I've ever had the privilege to unite."

Trent smiled down at Lana, his arms full of their daughter, his eyes full of love.

"Thank you, Mrs. Montgomery," he said.

"For what?" she asked.

"For loving me," he said, "for teaching me how to love."

"Oh, cowboy," she said as she grabbed his tie and pulled his lips down to hers, "you haven't seen anything yet."

* * * * *